TALES FROM THE CHILDREN OF THE SEA

Book One

THE LAST WOODEN HOUSE

by
Jann Burner

"REMEMBER WHO YOU ARE.
REMEMBER WHO YOU WERE.
REMEMBER WHY YOU CAME"

Chapter Titles

1. "And So It Is"
2. "Harry's Dream"
3. "Desire, Fascination & The Proposition"
4. "The Woodchopper of Happy Valley"
5. "The Wall, The Monday War & General Havoc"
6. "Random Cause I"
7. "Random Cause II"
8. "The Imagination & The White Knight"
9. "And"
10. "And Part II"
11. "The Cave of Nth Degree"
12. "Asher & the City of Light"
13. "A Pretender in Paradise"
14. "Faith, Speculation & the Bridge"
15. "The Time Traveler, the Standing Dead & the White Dolphin"

Prologue

By 2014 hundreds of men and women were observed cruising the coastal waters between Alaska and the Sea of Cortez. In the summer of the year 2015 U.S. Coast Guard spotters in Northern California observed seven hundred kayaks pass Point Reyes headed South. The emergence of these *Sea Gypsies*, as described by the media of the day, can be explained in part by the Crash of '09' which drove a failing economy over the edge and sent untold millions to the streets and to the woods in search of work, food and personal freedom. For a lot of people on the coast at this time the initial step off onto the sea seemed most natural. For a minimal initial investment they found essentially unlimited freedom. With a well outfitted ocean kayak they were tied to neither gas station, welfare office or complex industrial technology.

At first the small boats were almost unnoticed upon the bays and inlets of Washington, British Columbia and California, mostly they belonged to day trippers out for a frolic in the sun. But, as their numbers grew, the more adventuresome began to take to the unprotected waters of the coasts, intent upon duplicating and expanding upon the adventures of those early, near legendary cruisers like Romer, Lindemann, Caffyn, Dyson, Gillet and many others too numerous to mention. Eventually some hearty souls began to actually live on the water, travelling the coastal shoals, obtaining their protein from the ocean as well as the coastal forests and the remainder of their nutritional needs from the new seaside gardens.

Suddenly there was a new breed of savage. Usually college educated, these kayakers equipped with fish line and snorkeling gear became the gypsies of the sea. With the introduction of cheap water makers in the early nineties and small solar-powered auxiliary motors by '08', many individuals began to complete the entire circuit between Glacier Bay and The Bay of Conception, on the East coast of the Baja peninsula, within a year and a half. This activity was called *Coasting* and these adventurers referred to themselves as *The Children of The Sea*.

By 2014 there would be observed isolated camp fires burning far into the night upon the more remote beaches of the Western coast of the Americas. And seated around these fires would be the most diverse group of individuals ever assembled outside of a war. Mountain trekkers, river runners, campers and back-country specialists of many kinds, gold miners from Alaska, taxi drivers and Dead Heads from San Francisco, poverty stricken musicians, aerobic instructors, hod carriers, college professors, NASA scientists and unemployed computer programmers, brought together by their love of the ocean, kayaking and the quest for personal freedom. Reminiscent of the mountain men of the previous century, these citizens wore suits of rubber instead of leather and had adopted ocean waves and swells instead of mountain ridges or desolate prairies as their roaming grounds. The original voyagers were usually loners and not terribly young, most having reached at least thirty years of age with many in their forties, and more than a few in their fifties as well. But within a few years entire families began to organize and travel, gathering each morning upon the beach beneath vibrantly colored flags denoting clan.

At first it was thought that the voyagers were merely following the weather patterns on their journey south, but some documents recently discovered in an old magazine point to the fact that they were following or traveling with dolphins on their path south. It is unknown who made contact first, the kayakers or the dolphins, but this early journalist states that specific dolphins and whales traveled with specific groups of kayakers, in order, it was thought, to show *The Children of The Sea* where the birthing grounds were located. In any case, the lesson bore fruit, and the first documented human birth in the sea took place in 2015, near the entrance to *Scammon's Lagoon* on the Pacific side of the Baja peninsula. The child was the now legendary *Mary Tree*. As near as can be determined, her mother became pregnant somewhere along the coast of Oregon. Later, many more salt water birth occurrences were reported and it became a matter of great pride to give birth to one's son or daughter in warm salt water while in the presence of dolphins and whales.

When this writer was a boy I remember my great-grandfather taking me aside one day to confide in me that he had been born in the Bay of Conception, in the shadow of a gray whale. My mother told me later that he had lied. Nonetheless, when he died he left me a strange artifact, which he referred to as his *Spirit Caller*. It was a piece of rippled tube about three feet long, said to be made from the intestine of a sea mammal and which, when swung about the head emitted an eerie sound. It was used (or so I was told) to signal to whales that a human birth was about to take place. The father would swing the spirit caller throughout the birthing process so that this might be the first sound heard by the newborn. The instrument would then be presented to the child as his or her very first earthly object. The child would carry it with him throughout his life to signal the birth of his own children and if all went well, eventually it's sound would be heard one last time to signal to the whales that a brother was leaving this earthly frame and he would be buried with his original Spirit Caller. Because my great-grandfather realized that he no longer lived among "*free*" *men*, he designated me as heir to his *Spirit Caller*. My parents smiled indulgently as he placed it in my young hand upon his death bed. But I have kept it all these years and it hangs now on the wall above my desk as I write. Someday perhaps I shall have the opportunity to summon a whale using my great-grandfather's instrument.

With a relatively small amount of money, a neophyte adventurer could purchase a perfectly fine seventeen foot ocean cruising kayak with separate bulkheads and a surface composed of fourth-generation solar cells with which to power his stereo, GPS unit or VHF transceiver. Many options were available. Later, of course, when the new child of the sea became more proficient, he or she would devise the means to obtain one of the new-generation clear glass kayaks. These were called *Crystal Ships*. Totally clear and essentially invisible in the water, they were made of a high strength but very light glass developed by NASA. These boats were utterly indestructible; one could land them on rocks without the risk of a scratch and they had a secondary quality which endeared them to their owners; they emitted a tone when struck with a solid object. Because each boat's sound was entirely unique, one lone kayaker could hail another over a long distance by merely striking the side of his boat with the handle of his paddle. Even in a dense fog a lone voyager could keep track of his fellow travelers by merely striking the side of his cockpit with his paddle while completing a stroke. In this way, one always knew where everyone was. Often a family or clan would order their boats tuned to specific tones and on long cruises, groups would click their cockpit combings in unison and send out a clear musical chord far across the water. Later on, the ritual of "*thumping the hull*" became very complex and individual clans would actually create their own music. One of my most prized possessions is an extremely rare CD of a kayaking clan celebrating a sunrise over Isla Espirtu Santo in the *Sea of Cortez*.

The Crystal Ships were very beautiful. They were utterly transparent. Empty on the water, they were invisible. At night, snap one cyalume light stick and lay it within the kayak and the boat would give off a soft colored glow as it slid through the water until dawn. The colored glow from the individual boats mixed with the crystal bell tone of a tuned hull could be awesome. Couple this with chanting and the whole gathering began to take on the look and sound of a Tantric chorus from God's own music hall moving on down multi-colored energy waves...across the great surround.

Since many of these *Children of the Sea* possessed gifts of spirituality and imagination, it was no surprise when hyperbolic tales began to emerge from around the glowing fires of these hi-tech aborigines. Through the process of speech they would share their ideas, concepts, mind pictures and fears as well as the random musings which come and go in the mind of the lone cruiser. The more interesting anecdotes were saved, reconsidered from time to time and embroidered upon, or edited and tightened much like fine short stories to be shared later with new friends on even more isolated beaches.

This pattern of speech, referred to as "*Speak*" or more usually "*Intuitalk*", was a technique whereby these sea gypsy's attempted to bypass the labyrinth of the intellect and speak directly and extemporaneously from the richness of what they called the *mind ground*. They even had a curious custom where they would interview their children as soon as the child began to speak.

They would ask the young human such things as--"Where did you live before you came here?" "What caused you to pass over in your last life?", "What did you do in your other life?" and "How do you know me?"

Apparently the parents were trying to establish a sense of serial continuity in the mind of the child so as to reduce the sense of alienation so common in their city brothers and sisters. These little intuitalk dialogues were of course recorded on a CD and given to the child to become part of his or her *Earth Kit* along with other important items like the previously mentioned *Spirit Caller*. This CD was intended eventually to be played beside the person's death-bed in the hope that listening to his or her own child voice describing the other side and another life would ease the transition for the now aged entity about to cross over. This entire recording process was referred to around their fires as the *Return to Earth Ceremony*. It would seem that we are all immortal *Light Beings* and everyone on Earth is an imperfect model striving towards perfection. This is a secret which we all hold in common.

These *Children of The Sea* had the custom of meditating while paddling. Asked why he meditated, one kayaker said he believed life was one connective matrix of meaningful coincidence-- synchronistic patterns that we have somehow isolated ourselves from. Meditation allowed him to fall back into that synchronistic web. He laughed and said that he felt he belonged to the *Church of Synchronicity*.

Within the extended cruising family clan citizen anthropologists have been able to isolate six specific levels of archetypal entities. First we have what we might call the simple *Thirty-Day-Adventurer* or tourist. These people usually traveled in a group under the watchful eye of a professional guide and the mere prospect of sleeping on the ground was viewed as an exotic event.

Second in this hierarchy was the *Writer-of-Words*, the individual who went on extended trips with the group and then sold his words and images to the societal herd through articles in books and magazines in order to finance his next adventure. It is this second level voyager that has proven to be our prime source of information. This particular type of vagabond was, often as not, a wolf of the steppes; too wild to ever be completely domesticated, somewhat alienated and unable to fit into normal society and yet too fearful to ever break completely free. This person was far too much of an addict to the fringe attractions of the urban scene like clean sheets, television, single's bars and good restaurants.

The third level of this anthropological stratification was typified by the *Cruising Jeweler*. This, our scientists now believe, was the first individual to totally break with the land and the mainland culture of the day. These individuals took a lesson from the Hopi and the

Navajo of the 19th Century and turned bits and pieces of silver and ivory and bone into items of personal adornment. They carried a minimum of supplies but still managed to turn out attractive as well as valuable works of art that we have all seen in museums. They traded their creations to the writer-of-words and sometimes to the thirty day adventurer and thus obtained the small funds they needed to survive.

The fourth level constituted the beginning of the shaman class. Here we find the famous *Scrimshaw Artists* who recorded legends and other magically significant images upon bone, ivory and tusk. The scrimshaw man (or woman) usually traveled alone for a good portion of the year and could be described as a co-creator and certainly a prime designer of the *Life Fable*, which is how the *Children of The Sea* viewed their earthly sojourn.

The fifth level of Coaster was the *Teller-of-Tales*, the *Catcher of Words*, the *Shape-Shift*; the true guru of the water. Sometimes this type of individual was referred to in legend as *Orca Man* because it is said that he was able to transform himself into Ornicus Orca--the killer whale, or as some people thought, he was an Orca who was able to transform himself into a man. The teller-of-tales or "*Stalker of Words*", or "*Word-Catcher*" always lived alone but sometimes came to the fires of traveling clan groups late at night to tell them stories and weave his magic. Some would accompany their stories with music or song but often as not they would simply rely upon the power and the magic of the spoken word. A *Teller-of-Tales* would recount strange and wonderful things to those gathered around the edge of the fire's glow.

The sixth and most obscure level of coastal cruiser was occupied by the entity known as the *Selkie*. This was reported to be a female presence only viewed dimly at sunrise or sunset. Never seen directly but only spotted from time to time in the fog or in the distance gliding away. To have encountered a Selkie was to have one's life transformed! The Selkie was a truly magical creature spending part of it's life as a seal (which ironically was food for the Orca) and part as a human, and when in human form it was said to be a female of such incredible beauty that all who chanced across her path fell in love in the deepest recesses of their being. The Selkie was said to often reside in the deep fjords of South East Alaska, and she was sometimes referred to as *Shadow* because that is usually the form in which she has been reported; a mere shadow slipping across a rock face deep in a glaciated canyon. The Selkie was--and some say still is--the link between this world of three dimensions and the world of the *original* children of the sea. She is said to come to certain men, like th*e Teller-of-Tales,* in their sleep and from that moment on their life fable unfolds in a most magical and mysterious fashion.

***

CHAPTER ONE

"And So It Is!"

Long after dark, long after we had pulled our kayaks high up on the beach South of San Francisco, in the shadow of the old World War II gun emplacements, the "*Catcher of Words*" appeared.

He seemed to materialize from out of the smoke from our driftwood fire. No one saw his boat, no one heard his approach. To those of us seated around the fire's warmth this was to be a very special evening. This night would become a treasured memory. This was the night that the "*Teller of Tales*" would speak of things yet to come. Of probable realities; of things that never were but might have been, and yet still could be.

He slowly drew our attention around the fire's glow with the motion of an Eagle's feather and as he began to speak in an alien dialect our mind's rose as one with the heat and the smoke of the idea…

"There was a young woman sitting on the edge of a cliff looking out to sea. There was light fog all around her. The sun was just beginning to rise over the horizon. She could feel the warmth on her back. In the distance there were nuclear explosions. It was a black and white image. It had become a black and white world. There were many explosions. In her mind's eye they resembled one vast slow motion montage of flowers blooming and this demonic floral display covered the entire earth.

"Her name was Asher. She described herself as an Angel with a broken wing. She saw her role as that of a witness. Who dropped the first bomb or to which side should go the final credit for ending the world was never determined. With the collapse of government and the total break-down of communication, all stops were pulled and everything that would explode, burn or even smolder was quickly thrown onto the great human conflagration. This last great charade was referred to by some, as the Rad-Wars, and by others…as the end of the world. In her wide blue eyes there were the reflections of many nuclear explosions, like tiny multiple irises.

"After the initial obligatory missile exchange, wolf packs of nuclear subs and doomsday satellites began to rain their destruction on anything that hummed, glowed or seemed to show any technological sign more advanced than the Stone Age. Within twelve months, the entire surface of the globe was plunged back into the Middle Ages, with a loose feudal structure holding the few cancer infected survivors together. Suddenly there was no more television, no radio, no money. In all the world there was not even one electric light.

"Her voice was a compassionate whisper and her tone was of one speaking to a lover in the dark. "And then the trees began to die." She said to no one in particular. "At first, no one noticed, and then it was too late. No more trees. Some speculated it was the radiation that killed the trees, others thought perhaps it was the shock of the successive nuclear blasts that killed them. One very wise old man was of a different mind. He said they died of a broken heart. It was a terrible sadness, he said, that made all the trees on earth whither and die". A single tear hung at the corner of her left eye, and then dropped silently into the gray ash that covered the ground.

"Wood became extremely rare. In the end, man's final quest was not for food nor even security or love; in the end, man's final quest was for wealth, and in the final days wealth translated as wood. Within a few years the last surviving wooden houses were disassembled board by board. The wealthy were seen to move about, from shadow to shadow, covertly displaying small chips of the extremely rare wood, crudely impressed in hastily melted plastic. Often these token bits of wood would be worn as a ring, bracelet, or pendant. In the end, it became a sign of status, rank and office. More importantly, though, the display of wood was a sign of greed and in the end, greed was the way of life, for a greedy man was a successful man; a greedy man was a survivor. In the very last days, a small chip of once-abundant pine wood was to be more valued than a truckload of the purest gold!

"The scene as viewed through Asher's eyes seemed almost like newsreel footage from another time. A time of utter destruction. There were few survivors and those few seem to flit about like mad insects, tearing houses apart for their wood and killing each other with casual abandon. But the final days were mercifully short. By the end of the 21st Century the last human survivors were finally destroyed by radiation-caused cancers and oxygen starvation. As the years passed, one after the other, silently, without the sound of human laughter, or the cry of human desperation, it was almost as if the mere idea of a human being was a dream, or worse…a *rumor*.

"The fog was beginning to lift as the sun moved higher in the early morning sky. Looking back over Asher's shoulder there was nothing but utter waste for as far as the eye could see. The nuclear blooms had long ceased and all looked…dead.

"For humans", continued Asher, "these were no longer the dark hours; for humans, the light, like a candle flame, finally flickered and went out. In the end, at the very last, the few remaining humans went out like a string of defective lights…on Christ's own tree."

"Down below, in the distance, there was something moving in the water. As the fog finally cleared, a group of dolphins could be seen closing with the shore.

"The celebration was finally over, the experiment was complete, and it was time for the evolutionary train to move on to the next station.

"For many, many years, there was silence, except for the terrible winds and the incessant flitting of insects. Then, finally, through an evolutionary surge brought about by the Rad-Wars, another group of intelligent creatures, this time from the sea, assumed their position as the dominant species. These new creatures were in fact much older than humans but were heretofore content to occupy a peripheral role in the cosmological drama until the sudden increase in radiation forced them to center stage.
The group of dolphins continued towards the shore and as they closed with the land a large white dolphin could be seen in the lead.

"And though the footprint of man was no longer to be found anywhere upon the earth, the dominant species, in their wisdom, chose to preserve certain artifacts and curiosities. One of these human creations, thus preserved, was an ancient wooden house. This building was called a Victorian and this particular city-site was once known in ancient times as San Francisco.

"The ancient wooden house stood perched on a high hill above the sea like an ancient bird of prey. It stood utterly by itself--

isolated, but in good repair, in spite of the fact that neither road nor path nor trampled grass gave evidence of habitation. It stood poised, almost alert. At one time, it was but one of thousands of such structures that dotted the avenues of the ancient city, the result of a truly explosive outburst of creative energy. This energy was able to translate the optimism of the day into standing constructions of wood and glass.

"These human constructions depended upon the principal of opposition and contrast. These human structures were very much the same as the structure of humans. They were one and all extremely eclectic, emotional, and unpredictable. They were all flow and movement, light and shadow: an architectural dance designed to entice the eye and captivate the mind. "

***

CHAPTER TWO

"Harry's Dream"

They were sailing; a knife in the water, cutting through the great surround. They were moving at speed. They were like a chord, an arpeggio, a mosaic, a fine weaving of consciousness--a carpet with a thousand hand-tied thoughts per inch. They were a coat of many colors. They were here for a purpose and they were in for a treat. How many of them were present was hard to tell. Certainly more than a few. It felt like a goodly number. At least eighteen. This was a sizable gathering.

They were warm-blooded creatures of great intelligence and they were riding a wave of realization. They were the wave come up from the deep. They were the new dawn about to break upon the world. They had come from the sea for a look around. But especially they had come to laugh, for of all the creatures in the universe, only one could actually laugh aloud. That one creature was once warm-blooded, smelled funny and called itself Man. Of course, there were those whose entire existence was but one long happy thought, but Man was the only creature that at one time could actually laugh aloud. Mankind was also the only species in the universe who thought itself alone. Perhaps this accounted for its cry of laughter.

On this evening, for it was indeed dark, with neither moon nor fading light of day to illuminate the scene, there were numerous candles burning in the parlor of the last wooden house. These candles hung from the ceiling and were part of what the humans once called a chandelier. This specific chandelier was constructed from the finest rock crystal, imported at great expense from a distant land, and ground and cleaved by expert craftsman so that the merest hint of light might be caught, trapped, and reflected throughout the room.

Directly beneath the ornate assemblage of dangling crystal, stood a very thin and frail looking creature; it looked like a human female of maximum years. She peered about the large, apparently empty, room with wide, pale blue eyes full of much intelligence and humor. When she spoke, it was as if her tender voice was coming from a long way off.

"Good evening, ladies and gentlemen," she said with a quiet whisper and a slow smile.

Small pools of laughter exploded around the empty room like hot glass marbles dropped into a vat of liquid nitrogen. It was a curious statement. It was meant to be funny--"Good evening ladies and gentlemen!" It was what they used to call a joke, an attempt at earthly humor. It appealed to the sense of the ludicrous and the incongruous for, in fact, no one in the entire room had ever been a lady or a gentleman. No one present had ever been human and yet here they were about to undergo the experience, to take the trip. But this was to be only a short trip, a mere two-hour sojourn, a simple tour of the last wooden house in San Francisco.

"And so we begin," continued their gentle guide.

"Once upon a time, long ago and far away, far beyond the shores of ignorance, far even beyond the dense jungle of imagination, in the midst of what was once called the Pacific Ocean, lay a large forested island known in those ancient times as Califia. And upon this almost legendary island there was a most miraculous city and this city was called by name--San Francisco. During these ancient times, the city of San Francisco was renowned as a place of eternal youth, which is not to say that the inhabitants were immortal, but rather, through strange mystic practices, they were able to maintain a youthful spirit even while their bodies grew old. People came from all over the world to admire the beauty and style of life within this area. It was not a city of industry, factories, or slums, but a city of artists, poets, small shopkeepers, and others of romantic persuasion. In those olden times, in order to gain access to this truly beautiful city, one was obliged to sail beneath a bridge of solid gold, which separated a natural bay from the open ocean.

"This Golden Gate connected the city of hills, which was San Francisco, with the oldest forest on the planet. The trees in this forest grew for thousands of years and reached such gigantic proportions that they blocked the sun from touching the ground, casting the floor of the forest into eternal darkness. Aboriginal legend tells us that in order to see the top of one of these giants, one would have had to lay flat upon the ground. And in the entire world, these miraculous trees of redwood grew only upon the coast of ancient Califia. This house that we now occupy was constructed with bits and pieces of ancient wood from the red trees."

Sighs were felt around the room, for the late 19th and early 20th centuries were exciting periods in the development of human consciousness, and everyone had heard tales about the red giants and the city of San Francisco.

"You may be wondering what a tour of this house will be like. Well, it will be rather like a poetry reading, for in the final analysis, what is a tree, if not a slow poem. And what are houses, if not frozen emotions and attitudes--thought forms brought through the organic stream and then dried, tied, cut, sectioned and fitted into place. Finally, entire sheets of melted sand were stood in place across the large openings so that the humans, who once resided within the confines of these marvelously artificial caves, might peer out at the surrounding natural world with confidence, marvel at its excitement and its danger, and feel safe and secure.

"Within these special zones of frozen emotion lay mystery upon mystery. The entryways were often paneled in rich mahogany, Zebra wood, walnut, or redwood stained a deep purple-brown. Within the rooms were little hidy places, where skins from once living creatures were stretched and stitched to form pads and cradles onto which the tired human might lay his or her fleshy body for a while, perhaps in order to escape the oppressive weight of earthly gravity. Scattered about the rooms could be found bits and chunks of aged wood, slabbed and polished so as to form boxes for containing and concealing treasures and collections. Other surfaces were designed solely for the display and ingestion of food. And, distributed throughout the house, were green plants. Green, growing things were to be found everywhere-- stuffed in corners, hanging from ceilings and even perched on newel posts. There were ferns of all types and palms and exotic varieties of bamboo. In the most lavish houses, whole rooms were constructed of glass and filled with living greenery. All this was done so that the occupants might forget for awhile that they were imprisoned within a maze of hard, angled surfaces, frozen emotions and rigid attitudes.

"Such was their desire to split things apart and categorize them that they even had individual names for their box-like rooms. There were 'living rooms,' 'bedding rooms' and 'resting rooms'. In the larger, more ornate, houses there were even special rooms set aside for ingesting the smoke from smoldering herbs, while other rooms were used solely for a game called billiards in which grown men would use long thin rods of wood to push small balls around a cloth-covered, slate-topped table.

"While the men gathered to ingest smoke from burning weeds and pester small, glossy balls, the ladies of the house often sat together in what was called the 'morning room.' Here they would chat, drink tea and create large complicated patterns of knots out of simple balls of string.

"These people, as a race, spent thousands of years within the confines of flat, angled surfaces. They spent so many generations within these houses, that eventually, the very insides of their minds began to take on the smell and character of wood. In the healthier humans, there was reported to be the faint odor of cedar and pine and redwood, while in the general mass, there was said to be nothing but the smell of plywood, particle board and mildew. In certain areas of society, their lives eventually became so artificial and so removed from any natural base, that there was rumored to be no odor at all. It was as if their entire existence were merely a surface impression photographically reproduced so as to represent the real thing."

She gracefully turned beneath the chandelier and gestured towards a crystal punch bowl situated at the very center of an ornately carved oak table in the middle of the room.
"And now," said their guide, somewhat breathlessly, as if

embarrassed by her own bold suppositions, "if you will..."

The bowl contained eighteen small, circular wafers: there were nine blue and nine pink. The wafers were exactly three inches in diameter and looked not unlike small slicks of oil compressed between thin sheets of plastic. They were good for two hours. These colors, pink and blue, were for gender: male, blue and female, pink. These particular dream wafers were further classified according to density of color. The darker the color, the older the earthly impression. Hence, if an entity wished to be a young female human for the two hours it would take to complete the tour, then it would be wise for that entity to select a pale pink wafer. Conversely, if one desired to be an elderly male, one would select a very dark blue wafer. And on this particular evening there was to be a bonus, for the complete experiential record of the house was to be in the bowl. Not physically, of course, but among the pile of dream wafers was one particular disc, imprinted with the entire history of the ancient house and of everyone who had at one time lived within its hard angled surfaces.

"Come, come now!" exclaimed their little old guide, clapping her hands together for emphasis. "Let us quickly make our selections and get physical! We don't have all day, as they used to say..."

Soon the dream wafers were spinning and twirling about the candle-lit room like small, colorful birds and within a twinkling, the guide's attempt at earthly humor was greeted by earthly smiles as nineteen people of various ages, sex and styles of dress stood, where just seconds before there had been but one. They looked as if they had just stumbled in off a charter bus or perhaps off an old aeroplane. They had that dazed look of conventioneers, newly arrived in a strange city, and this impression was reinforced by the fact that each and every one wore a rather large, plastic name tag neatly pinned over their heart.

Of the nineteen, one entity, appearing as a rather elderly man in dark, conservative dress, stood off by himself trying to conceal the hint of a smile. In this guise, he was a large man and the grey suit that he wore appeared to have, at one time in the distant past, hung upon an even larger man. The white plastic name tag on his chest identified him simply as "*HARRY*." As Harry, his face had a dusty, almost deathly pallor that fitted perfectly the ambience established by the darkness of the stained-wood eating room. His thinning, long grey hair hung low over his large ears in silent testimony to ancient times when things and fashions were different. He would have walked unnoticed through the ancient streets of San Francisco had it not been for his eyes.

His eyes were brilliant, flashing green, and looked as out of place upon his old weathered face as emeralds in the hand of a street beggar. He slowly walked over to the window and ran a wrinkled old finger along the sill as if testing for dust. His nostrils flared and his mind began to spin as he drank in the ancient odor of the place. He glanced around the room at the others. Without anyone having to tell him, he knew that his dream wafer was the ONE. He suddenly knew the house of redwood...intimately. He could scarcely contain his excitement. As their guide continued to speak, he shook his being through the memory frame that once constituted the building's total experience and reeled from the emotional impact. Kaleidoscopic patterns of pure memory and sensation swept over him. It was a vertiginous feeling as his mind began to spill feelings and images like water in an overfull bucket. He grasped the edge of the window frame to keep from falling. He glanced around quickly, seized by what humans once called *paranoia*. No one had noticed. They were all too busy checking out their new bodies. They were like children trying on their parents' clothes. They viewed this new experience as funny and fascinating.

"Oh, yes, yes!" cried one.

"My my, I didn't realize that this was how it was going to be!" uttered another.

"Crazy me, crazy me. Just look at these hands, these fingers! Look at the way they...move!"

"Oh these eyes...what fun!" said one young lady, as she turned around, ever-so-slowly, taking in the others while at the same time watching her own reflection in the surface of a large mirror across the room above the mantle.

One man, around forty, fingered the fiber of his fine wool suit and stared in awe at the crystal display from the chandelier. "*The light*," he said quietly, "look at the way it...sparkles!"

According to the unspoken rules tourists were always to appear in appropriate costume when visiting an ancient historical site, but in the case of a Victorian house, this loose edict resulted in one man in a pale blue leisure suit standing next to an older woman wearing a Victorian gown, while across the room stood an authentic American cowboy speaking in low tones to a young blonde in a beehive hairdo and a green mini-skirt.

"Oh yes, yes, yes," said the young girl in the mini to the cowboy. "Isn't this simply marvelous, one instant we were something else in an entirely different space and now we are Humans--*being*."

And then they all laughed because, after all, laughter was why they had come.

As Harry, the old man found himself knowing many things about the house constructed out of redwood. It was a many-faceted house. Depending upon one's position, the dwelling seemed to take on the qualities that the observer held to be important. At one point, it was a new house, as lithe, trim and slim as a newly constructed sailing sloop. It was, on the whole, a contented house, serving its occupants far longer than most, and with a cheerfulness and enthusiasm not usually expected, nor anticipated, from working class dwellings. It was a brown suit in a closet of many colors; serviceable and dependable, with just the slightest hint of fancy stitching along the seams.

Harry knew, for instance, that the house had been originally constructed for Lucy Stone by her husband. But then, less than a year after its completion, Lucy had been killed by a runaway horse and wagon. Lawrence Stone sold the house at that point and moved on. It next became a sort of halfway house for young school teachers on tour of the Western states, as well as for latecomers, newly arrived from the East or just returned from the gold fields of the Yukon. Later, during World War I, it was divided into different units and served as a boarding house for doughboys awaiting rides out into foreign places to meet their destiny.

During the "other war" (the second one), an old German man had lived in the lower rooms. He had once been a famous photographer in prewar Germany, but by then was forced to eke out a marginal living, taking pin-up pictures of loose young ladies which he would then sell to soldiers passing through the city on their way to the Pacific Theater.

Harry also learned, for instance, that during the "Fifties," the neighborhood in which the house stood began to slip and the building was filled, year 'round, with bohemian artists and self-indulgent writers with their heads full of sand.

During the middle "Sixties", the house was the lair of a wealthy, LSD-crazed drug dealer who finally met his demise in the balcony of a theater in the neighborhood. Later, there was a quick succession of colorful characters. There was a bottomless dancer and a taxi driver. They watched a lot of television, laughed, snorted cocaine and ate only natural food. Next, there was a string of young singles and divorced suburbanites fresh to the *Magic City* and intent on carving out a new life.

Finally, the entire neighborhood, which had been tottering for years, tilted to the left and collapsed into total disrepair. The space downstairs was transformed into a Chinese laundry. The top flat was leased to a convalescing transsexual. The front room was occupied by three armed Zionists and the two side rooms were rented to an attractive young, big breasted hustler named Candy whose twelve-year old dwarf son made his living training tarantulas for guard duty in the town's better jewelry salons.

"And now, if you'll follow me..." cooed their guide with a suppressed chuckle, turning and striding off down the long hall. Harry smiled, too, and slid into control of his new body, like a man at the controls of an exotic machine. He fell into line as they all began to file off like a bunch of innocent children on their way to class--eyes bright and shinning. And in a very real sense, they were a bunch of children on their way to school, and once again it was to be the very first day and everything was...*new*.

"On your left, ladies and gentlemen, is what was once termed the bathing room. The large ceramic container on the right is where the ancient ones would deposit their envelopes of flesh for ritual cleaning. It is here that they would come for purification, for the removal of the residual dirt and grime, both physical as well as psychical, that would be acquired through movement in the world. The large container on the left, in which the body was left to soak was filled with water (something with which you are all very familiar) while the smaller ceramic bowl on the floor in the rear is where it is believed they prayed."

Chuckles were heard from her group of men and women crowded around in the bathing room, for they knew that this last comment by their guide was another attempt at earthly humor and humor was honored and appreciated above all other human tendencies.
"Actually, it is believed that one was supposed to place one's nude body upon the device, as if in a chair..."

"Ooh's" and "Ah's" were heard from the group as they grasped the real purpose of the strange device.

"...and by concentrating upon one's minor place within the overall scheme of things, ones negative residual emotions would somehow solidify and finally pass on out of the body physical.

At that point, one would be obliged to pull the long, metal chain to the left which would activate a stream of fluid from the holding tank above. This water would flow down into the ceramic bowl and both dilute and flush ones bodily waste down through the opening in the floor and hopefully back unto the source from which all things originate."

Individual members of the tour nodded and looked to one another with sly winks. The ancient ones certainly were clever. Had a definite sense of style.

"And now, if you'll follow me..."

Sounds of swishing skirts and smooth skin scraping against the hard celluloid of starched collars underlined their amazement and accompanied the group down the long dark hall. Rather abruptly, their guide stopped and turned, pointing down at a small metal grate recessed within the surface of the wooden floor.

"Below this surface upon which we are standing, in what was once referred to as the basement, stands a giant, cavernous, black metal container into which the ancient ones would stuff their disposable combustibles. By thus altering the molecular structure of these disposable items, sufficient heat energy was generated to warm the entire living structure."

The cowboy immediately dropped to his knees in order to peer through the metal grating in hopes of catching a glimpse of the thing that ate disposable combustibles. It was extremely dark and he was mildly disappointed.

At this point, Harry turned and slowly moved off, for he intuited a secret in this house and he sensed that the secret was to be found somewhere in the rear sleeping room on the very lowest level. He deftly descended the stairs unobserved and passed through numerous rooms and anterooms, with all the familiarity of a long term resident until he finally came to the special room.

It was a small, cheerless, grey room and the mood established by the grayness was cracked by the sun baked, once-red corduroy drapes that hung now like flimsy stencils admitting selected beams of diffused moonlight to shine softly through the paintless patterns and onto the far wall, across from the open doorway. Harry entered slowly and slid his attention around the small room and over its dusty surfaces of dark wood like a thin layer of paint. His eyes continued to scan the room for details. He felt like a restless gunfighter from out of the *Old West*.

With slow but sure movements, he edged across the finely-fitted hardwood floor towards the place of fire. It was a beautiful structure. The fire box itself was covered with gold metal filigree depicting forest scenes from the mythos of ancient man. Surrounding the fire box was a wide background of shiny, lime green, ceramic tiles. At the outward edge of the tiles was a white wooden frame and this frame was in turn flanked by two substantial wooden pillars. These two pillars supported a mantle piece and this in turn supported two smaller pillars which served as a foundation for a somewhat smaller wooden shelf. And between these two shelves, at eye level, was a large, oval reflecting surface once called mirror by humans.

Harry raised a hand tentatively and gently slid it along the leading edge of the lower mantle piece. A small strip of exotic wood moved with a distinctive "click". Of all the thousands of pieces of individual wood, this one particular strip seemed to hold the secret. He leaned against the mirror momentarily for support and found himself gazing into a stranger's face. Harry had never seen a mirror before coming to this house. He almost didn't recognize himself. He thought that the face looked unnecessarily severe, almost criminal, but then he remembered that human nature was a prairie for outlaws.

For reasons which he never fully understood Harry placed his hands on the cool reflecting surface and pushed. It moved. It was designed to swing. Without a moment's hesitation, he slid his fingers into the opening, volunteers on a dangerous mission. In the open space behind the mirror was a container--a box of some sort. He slowly removed it from the confines of its dark, secret place and put it on the bed across the room. The container was created from the treated skin of some long extinct animal. It was a dark, rusty brown in color--one of those old boxes that men used to drag around whenever they left home on foraging trips in search of money.

To say that he was excited at his discovery would be a gross understatement. He was literally beside himself. He sat on the bed and gingerly snapped open the small silver clasps, and carefully tilted back the stiff upper lid. Inside the ancient brown leather suitcase, nestled within a softly vibrating blue ring, lay a small clear bowl. So, Harry thought, this is the secret. He carefully lifted the small bowl toward the light for closer inspection. There was something moving in the bowl. At first, in the shadows, it looked like small, brilliantly colored tropical fish, but no, these were more fluid than any fish; more ephemeral than a slick of oil upon the water. The quick, brilliant colors and swift dartings almost made him look away. So bright, so colorful, so intense, he thought. Always emerging, never defined, ever unfolding, never completely caged within any context. There could be no doubt. These were concentrated thought drops. This was a miracle! This was an ancient container of *Human Dreams*.

Upon closer examination, he could spot certain differences. Here were night dreams as well as day dreams. What a find. A bowl of dreams, small patterns of human spiritual energy, invested with emotion and content which gave the individual bits their specific color, hue, and intention. The brightest, shimmery ones were obviously the night dreams whereas the duller, semi-opaque, slower moving ones were probably the day dreams: products of idle contemplation and bored minds. This was mankind's protector, its cushion. Dreams protected mankind from reality, the same as the embryonic sack protected the unborn fetus within the womb.

There had been rumors and faint, whispered thoughts referring to such things passed from one mind to another but never, never did he suspect that such a thing actually existed in physical form. These were no dream wafers, no limited two-hour sojourn through a socially sanctified city-site. These were the things from which Universes were created...and *Minds*.

There was only one thing to do. Without a moment's hesitation, Harry moved the small, clear container to his mouth. With a quick snap of his head and a smack of his lips, he drank the entire mix as if it were mere water and he a man suffering from extreme dehydration. He stood and walked over to the mirror. In its silvery reflective surface, he observed one small, shimmering droplet hanging uncertainly from a dark grey, follicled whisker at the very edge of his upper lip. He flicked his tongue, lizard-like, and caught the stray dream droplet that hung so precariously before it could fall to earth. He shook his head and moved unsteadily to replace the container behind the mirror once again. So quick, he thought. As his body moved to lift the container, his mind began to radiate dreams--*human dreams*. And, because he was old, he dreamed of youth, and because he was in an ancient city, he dreamed of a country place, and because his life thus far, had been relatively dull and uneventful, he dreamed of adventure and excitement.

"Oh, what flowers of delight!" he said aloud.

And with this, there was a subtle "*click*," as from the opening of a backdoor, as from the opening of a human mind, and with this, the rings of realization began to radiate in all directions across the pond of time.

***

CHAPTER THREE

"Desire, fascination and the proposition"

There was an old man clad in rags, seated at the very edge of the forest, at the border where the plain of *Tranquility* runs up hard against the dense forest of *Content*. He was a tired-looking creature with long, white wind-whipped hair seated upon the close-cropped grass of the forest floor.

"What is this?" Harry wondered, approaching the old man seated in the grass at the edge of the trees.

The elderly gentleman watched Harry approach from out of the twinkling corner of one half-closed, emerald green eye. As he drew closer, the old gray beard nodded and slowly turned his body to greet him and smilingly replied to his unspoken question.

"I am the Geni of Desire, young man, and I dwell at the edge of the Forest of Content, that's <u>*Content*</u>, young man, not content." I see by your name-tag that you are called Harry. May I call you Harry? Fine, I'll call you Harry."

Harry was embarrassed to see that he was still wearing the large, white plastic name tag from the tour. He made a move to remove it.

"No, no, leave it," said the old man. "It serves you well. Now please sit. Sit down here in front of me."

Harry did as he was told. He seated himself directly in front of the stranger and marveled at the words which seemed to slip from the weathered, old face like gaseous balloons and rise gracefully, spreading their gentle energy across the warmish, summer sky. He noted that what first appeared to be merely old rags were actually the remnants of an ancient costume, part circus, part military, with stripes and faded spots, tattered epaulets, faded badges and metallic signs of rank and position. And, lying in the grass, close by, was a small, hand-crank organ once used by traveling circus performers. The old musical device was faded from its time under the sun and its once colorful inscriptions were now almost illegible. From the side of the Geni's ancient organ ran a long, silver cord and at the very end of the cord was a small, costumed monkey attached by a tiny leather collar. He was sitting about ten feet away, holding a small, engraved silver cup and openly observing them both.

"Who is your friend?" Harry inquired.

The old Geni rocked back and forth, hugging himself in great appreciation of the moment and began to chuckle.

"My little friend's name is *Fascination* and he, too, lives at the edge." Desire stretched out his hand to Fascination, who leaped up laughing, and turned towards Harry frantically shaking his little, silver, engraved monkey cup.

"Is Fascination thirsty," Harry inquired, observing the empty cup, "or hungry? For if he is, we can go to the house which is not far away..."

"Forget the house, Harry," interrupted Desire. "It is further away than you can imagine and, no, Fascination is not thirsty because he does not drink and he is not hungry because he does not eat. He is merely anxious that you give him some small token of your affection."

"But what can I offer your friend? I have no worldly goods, no things, no toys, no 'stuff'?"

The Geni lit a small, curved cobbler's pipe and slowly expelled a stream of smoke between his yellowed teeth, saying in a strong, breathy whisper, "You have hope, my friend. All he needs is a little *Hope*."

"Well, then, you've got it! You can have all the hope I can muster--you and your little friend there."

Old Desire nodded and smoked and slowly rocked back and forth. "That's good. That's good. Hope in exchange for my services." He smiled. "You're leaving on a journey this day, Harry, a very important journey. This will undoubtedly be the most important journey of your life. And whenever someone leaves on a journey, they need a place to put their hope. So, I'll make you a deal. Place your hope with *Desire* and *Fascination*, Harry, and you will have the power to...*DREAM*!" The old graybeard suddenly raised his arms high into the air and with a grand Geni-like flourish, continued with his pronouncement. "I hereby give you *The Wish*, my young friend. Whatever you wish for, or indeed, even feel the need to bring into the jungle of your imagination will be validated, authenticated and made...***REAL***."

Harry couldn't help but wince at the resonant sound of the old man's pronouncement. He wasn't quite sure if he liked the rather ponderous, fateful quality of the words. As he watched, the Geni picked up his ancient instrument and sent his fingers scurrying over its keyboard, creating fantastic music, while Fascination ran around in excited circles shaking his little silver cup and jabbering in monkey talk.

"You must go to the wilderness." The words came unexpectedly like lyrics to a long forgotten song.

"But why?"

"You must come to see the face you wore before you looked in the glass..." exclaimed the Geni.

Harry felt confused. The graybeard looked at him and winked. "There is much to learn that is not yet spelled out in letters." And then he stopped playing. "But remember, Harry, the words, the musical notes, the beautiful noise, is just the rattling of bones. It is the pauses, the pools of silence that are important. The words merely alert the listener to the depth of the pool. Humans are a telepathic bunch, Harry, and the ones who are unafraid, like large spaces and deep pools."

Desire set down his organ and relit his pipe, holding the flame up for Harry to see. "Want to see something exciting? Some real communication? Wait until you see some of the deep trollers sing their songs, tell their sad and wondrous stories around a fire! It is electric! Something to do with the flame. Guaranteed to make you feel absolutely still..." He blew out the flame.

"Yes, I would like that. I would like someday to play an instrument like you. I wish to play the separate moments of my life like individual notes of music. To be able to compose my days like a progression of musical chords, a series of compositions around a central theme...that would be something!"

"And that day shall come to pass, my young friend. But, if you wish to orchestrate your consciousness, you must remember to give it your full attention. Here..." said the Geni.

He offered up a small intricately embroidered sack.

"Is this for me?"

"For traveling and adventuring," whispered Desire into the right side of Harry's mind. "This is to be a mystery tour, and within this small sack is found almost all the magic you will need."

Harry plunged his hand into the plush material and pulled forth a small pipe of silver, ivory, and bone. Etched deeply into the silver were three words--*DESIRE, HOPE* and *TRUST*. Below these three words, stretching completely around the small ivory bowl, was a white dolphin arching high above the waves of the ocean.

"Desire something worthy Harry, hope for the best, and trust that it will all work out."

Harry gently replaced the pipe deep within the folds of the small sack upon its bed of finely chopped possibility and shredded expectation.

Desire stood and slowly began to pace back and forth.

"Now, about this journey of yours, Harry. I am afraid there will be no turning back. You may choose to stop at some point during the course of the journey, but you may never turn back." The old man hesitated for a long moment considering his words. "This trip is sure to be wildly dangerous, but you are now a young man and you have vision. I suspect that with a little bit of what we call luck, you may eventually reach the very source of the mystery."

Harry felt slightly dizzy. Once again he didn't like the Geni's tone. "What do you mean by--*luck*?"

The old gray beard placed his index finger to his chin for a moment and reflected before answering. "Good question, Harry. *Luck* is that little creature that lives in the space between *trust* and *doubt*. It is like the little electrical spark that leaps across two synapses in your brain when you wish your finger to move, and trust that it will, and then observe it actually move! It is a little miracle."

Harry had to smile. "Yes, the little miracle. I can see that. But what is this mystery that you speak of?"

"Well, first I must speak to you of the *Big Sea*. Beyond this tranquil plain, far and away even beyond the *Forest of Content*, even beyond the dense *Jungle of The Imagination* lies what is called by name the *Big Sea*. Now, this idea is very large; it incessantly heaves its grand intention upon the beach of fractured dreams purely in order to reshape the shore of reality, and at the very exact and specific center of this ocean floats *The Muse*."

"And what is *The Muse*?" Harry inquired.

"The Muse," replied the old man, "is none other than **The Dreamer of All That Is.**"

"Of *All That Is*?"

"Yes!" replied the Geni.

Harry found this hard to believe. "Even the land that we stand on and the future that we imagine?"

"Even you and even me..."said Desire in a husky whisper.

Harry felt an old, vertiginous paranoia crawling up his spine. "I see," was all that he could say.

"Then rejoice in the realization that you do see. Listen to my words when I say that your apparently inexhaustible life will pass in the twinkling of an eye. It is but a series of imagined events in the mind of *The Dreamer*. The most that you can hope for is good company along the way."

For some reason Harry felt positively depressed. "I hear your words and see your meaning, but it makes me feel sad. Why should I continue on this dangerous and mysterious journey? To tell the truth it frightens me."

"Well," said Desire with a shrug, "what can I say? In order to become whole; in order to fulfill the destiny that is set before you, you must first spend some time being human, and journeys like this are what humans seem to do."

"But who am I to do such a thing? I don't think that being human is really part of my nature."

"The thing is often, if not always, more than the sum of its parts. Do not underestimate the qualities of Man. That creature who walked around calling itself human was seldom expressing more than twenty percent of the truth. Just below the surface rode an entity of awesome proportion. As a human, Harry, you are like an iceberg. You are cruising eighty percent beneath the water, with only the tip of what you are exposed to the sun and the wind."

"But why do I have to do this?"

"Because you have vision Harry, and because, at this moment, you are a human being. I am just an old thing named *Desire* and while Desire may grant vision, its wish to see, there is but one Dreamer and it is called by name **The Muse**: the first cause, the initial drop in the big pond, the very source of gravity.

"The sadness and fear that you feel, the desire that you feel, Harry, is nothing compared to the primal agony of the slumbering Muse, yearning for adequate proof of its own reality. And yet, from out of that pit of protracted primal yearning comes the dream of all that is. Likewise, from your own agonized yearning will emerge the dream of all that you are."

Harry was silent for a long while, digesting the information being fed to him. Finally, his imagination seized upon a question, "Has anyone ever seen the *Dreamer*?"

The old veteran slowly folded his hands one over the other. "It is said that only a great artist has even the slightest chance of ever encountering the Muse."

Harry found himself hunching forward in spite of himself, anxiously leaning on the Geni's every word. The Geni seemed to eye him with suspicion, furrowing his brows as if trying to burn sincere desire into his youthful human spirit.

"Now listen carefully to what I say, my young human friend."

Harry found himself nodding enthusiastically.

"An artist's goal is similar to that of the alchemist, except, that it is not gold he is after, but direct communication with the source. His quest is to become reabsorbed, re-indentified, and finally reunited once again with the *Dreamer of All That Is* in a single explosive instant!"

The *Geni of Desire* paused for a moment to re-light his pipe before continuing. "I have only known of one individual to have survived such an encounter and that particular human spoke to me of his quest, not in words, but in music. Through his personal song performed upon a stringed instrument, crafted with his own hands, he was able to form and shape the melody so that for the duration of the music I was with him and we were together with *The Muse*. The sounds that he generated that day were so awesomely beautiful that nearby residents of the countryside began to speak of the Artist and when our time was done and he moved on, these same neighbors were given to wearing great ecstatic smiles for the rest of their days."

Harry looked deep into the sparkling clarity of Desire's eyes and, for an instant, he was treated to a view of the infinite as it spread before them in all directions.

"You see, art is a bridge between spirits," said Desire. "You will become an artist"

"Is this something I want to do?"

"An artist cannot enjoy his life by evading his task, Harry. Look at it this way--art isn't a solo performance, it's a symphony in the dark, and you, as an artist, are merely an instrument registering something already existent. We are only instruments of a greater power, my friend."

Harry nodded and focused on his breathing.

The old gray beard sat down beside him and motioned with his hand toward the forest that spread out before them. Apparently a decision had been made and he was now ready to receive his final instructions.

"First," said Desire, "you must thoroughly explore *The Forest of Content* until it leads you to the dense, inner *Jungle of The Imagination*. Then, when you finally become totally lost within the jungle, create an instrument of music--for without a song in your heart you will surely remain lost in the imagination forever and a day. Beyond the jungle of your own imaginings, you will eventually discover a paradise, but beware, for it will not be your Paradise because true *PARADISE* is created--never discovered.

"If you are successful the Muse will eventually hear your song and she will send her messengers to lead you to the very edge of the Sea--the *Great Surround*! At this point if your song is pure and your direction is clear, she will become distracted and, little by little, your song will assume a larger proportion within the *Dream of All That Is*. Soon thereafter the currents found within will begin to move you, and then, if you are extremely lucky, you will see the white dolphin: he is the last messenger of the Muse."

Harry was exhausted just listening to this information.

"But, Desire, what if I make it to the Big Sea, but never encounter the white dolphin?"

The Geni looked slowly to his left and then to his right as if silently conferring with numerous invisible advisors.

"In that case you will either die of thirst or go slowly mad and land on the coast of ignorance in the land of was, during the days of future past, before the flood that is yet to come."

Harry felt sick. "That's it?"

The white haired old man raised his right index finger high into the air, as if testing for a celestial breeze. "That's it! No one returns once they attempt to sail the *Big Sea*!"

"No one?" he ventured.

"Nope. Not even the white dolphin."

"But what if I make it to the edge of the Big Sea and no further?"

"Then," said Desire, "you will become one of the standing dead and remain on the beach forever to gaze out over the ocean of fractured dreams like a once living statue."

"But the dense inner jungle of the imagination is so awesome and convoluted, surely I will become lost forever..."

The Geni looked most gravely at him.

"For sure, and forever and a day," he said sternly. "Unless you retain enough of your insight to create a musical instrument; for only through practiced performance upon an instrument of your own creation will you finally develop discipline and skill enough to find your way through the maze of your own most private imaginings."

Harry felt afraid. There was no way around it. "What if I don't create a suitable instrument and remain lost in the jungle?"

"Then," said the old man peering off into the distance, tapping the ends of his fingers together and uneasily reading Harry's mind, "you will become a Shaman and by your presence you will serve as a marker and guide for all those who may come after."

"But the Forest of Content is so very large and unfamiliar and I am new at being human. Surely with each new day I will find nothing but further distraction and complication."

Desire smiled for the first time in a long while, "Don't be so fearful, my young friend, for the *Forest of Content* is not unlike a forest of trees and while they may indeed run many in number, their specific variety is limited. Just remember that you are like an iceberg, Harry, and that everything you encounter is mere symbol. Remain thoughtful and please do not become so obsessed that you end up counting the leaves."

"I've got to tell you, Desire, what you are saying really scares me! I am but one person and what if I end up, as you say, lost in the Forest of Content counting the leaves on the trees?"

The old man cleared his throat, turned and casually dropped a small clear capsule into Harry's newly acquired adventuring bag.

"Then, Harry," he said with a wink, "you will end up just like everyone else."

So. Harry nodded and prepared to move off into the trees. Finally he understood. To be like everyone else was a compromise that he was unwilling to make. "And the small clear capsule? What is this for?"

"That," replied Desire with a quizzical expression, "is for no-thing and practice."

Harry turned and started off down the path into the woods. It was a sunny day. He was a human being and, once again, everything was...*new*.

***

CHAPTER FOUR

"The woodchopper from happy valley"

The *Forest of Content* was much more than a random grouping of bushes, shrubs, rocks and trees. It was a mini-continent with miles of gently blowing prairie grasses, wide open expanses of flat grassy tundra, tall stands of strong trees, dense verdant valleys, hot arid deserts, five oasis, three mountains and four major rivers. These rivers served as borders and helped shape and contain the constantly changing nature of the forest. They were called by name: Sirgit, Segnag, Setarhpue and Elin.

The path wound gradually upward into the trees. It was hard, climbing over logs, slipping on moss, getting caught on the thick brush and broken limbs. Harry stopped once to look back, but all he could see was a dense umbrella of tree tops below him. The path continued to steepen, spiraling up the mountain. Soon the dense valley vegetation began to thin, and there, interspersed with the trees, were large rock outcroppings where eagles perched eyeing him warily as he passed. Near the summit of the mountain he heard a strange sound and without hesitation, he strayed from his path.

Through the trees less than one hundred yards away he saw a short, stout man striking a large tree with much aggression. As Harry drew closer, he noted that the man was shirtless and that the entire upper portion of his body was covered with course black hair. In his hands, he held a wicked-looking axe. With this weapon, he was inflicting substantial damage upon a living tree. Being as unfamiliar with logging as he was with strangers, Harry approached, intending to voice his concern for the safety of the tree. Perhaps he could settle the dispute.

The woodchopper, watching Harry approach, ceased his activity and laid down his axe, for trees were easier to find in this territory than momentary companionship, and any interruption from work on such a warm day was welcome.

"How you doing, stranger?" sang out the wood chopper. "Hot enough for you?"

"I'm doing fine, my friend, but I am a little concerned about the tree."

The woodsman thought Harry's comment quite funny, and, as he laughed, he pulled a red handkerchief from his pants pocket, eagerly wiping the sweat from his face.

"How about a nice cold brew?" The man turned and walked over to his strange looking vehicle.

"What's that?" Harry asked, pointing towards the man's machine.

"What's this?" mimicked the man laughing. "Boy, you must be a stranger in these parts. This is my ATV, my horse, my transport, and my home away from home. She'll climb a sheer rock face, ford a river, or cross the swamp. She's the love of my life."

As the man pulled the two small cans from a small compartment on the side of his vehicle, Harry noticed a deep scar that ran down the left side of the man's face like a barren river bed.

"Bet you're wondering how I knew you were a stranger? Don't get many strangers anymore, except those who come to work on The Wall. I hardly think you're one of them kind. The last stranger I seen was back in '39 and he had come to fight in The War. But seeing as how there ain't no men allowed in the war no more, you must have another reason."

He eyed Harry suspiciously. "Say, why you wearing that silly looking name tag? 'HARRY,' that must be your name. So why do you have to wear the tag? Afraid you'll forget your name?" He laughed and swallowed his beer.

"Something like that." Harry liked the man in spite of his sarcastic tone. He tasted the canned drink. Beer. He liked it. It was surprisingly refreshing on such a hot day. They were standing near the top of the mountain, and through the spaces where the trees had been removed, Harry could see for miles and miles.

"Look over there," the wood chopper pointed, "on the other side."

Harry looked to where the trees gave way to rocks, the rocks to desert, and the desert finally to what looked like a swamp in the distance. Beyond the swamp was a thick veil of fog. In the middle distance was a large housing tract. It looked like hundreds of identical houses lined up one after the other, row after row.

"That's where I live," said the man with more than a hint of pride in his voice. "That's my home. We call it Happy Valley. If you're ever in town, stop by for a visit. It's an R-G-B development; you know, alternating rows of red, green and blue. No addresses, totally democratic. The red houses are the executives and managers, of course, the green are the technicians and the blue are the blue collar workers. I'm blue. Actually, I'm a technician, but my job classification is still blue collar. I'm a welder. I'm row nine. Just count twelve greens and the next blue is me." He stopped talking and picked up his axe. With a deft flip, it arced through the air once, twice--*SNUCK!*

"I'm into work. Woodchopper by day, welder by night." He stopped to recover two more cans of his strange brew. "Gotta keep busy. Work, work, work! Here, have another beer."

"Work," Harry mused aloud. "I don't work."

"Say, what kind of weirdo are you? You're a man, you work! Simple enough. That's what men do. To live is to work, to work is to live. We're after progress here, and in order to progress, we must change; and in order to change things we must work. Our elders tell us we must invent; we must alter; we must hurry! We must quickly create a totally man-made environment. Before nature takes over. That's one of the reasons I'm a woodchopper. We must sever our ties with nature. Get rid of all this stuff," he motioned around towards all the trees and bushes and flowers. "Damn things just harbor bugs and disease."

"And who is responsible for these...ideas? Who is your master architect?"

"The elders, of course. Listen, you sound like you didn't get properly educated! "

"But the Dreamer of All That Is has created a wondrous universe for you to play in...if he is satisfied, how is it that you're not?"

The woodchopper retrieved his axe from the tree and looked over at him disapprovingly.
Harry continued, "Maybe your elders are just dragging you along towards an unknown and unhealthy destination?"

The woodsman had seemed to tire of their discussion and hitched up one of the freshly severed trees behind his machine with a length of chain and prepared to start off down the mountain toward his home in Happy Valley.

"I agree with you on one thing, boy. Our elders are dragging us along the road as surely as I am about to drag this log, but I do not agree that they are dragging us towards an unknown destination. I am dragging this log down the mountain to my home where I am going to cut it up into small pieces and burn it in my stove and heat my house. I damn sure know where I am going and I am sure that our elders are pulling us toward a purposeful place they are sure of, too.

"Listen, kid, I don't know where you come from and I don't think I even want to know, but let me give you some advice. If you plan on staying around these parts, you'd better get a job! Get two jobs and look for a third on your free time. If you don't, somebody, could even be me, is going to report you to the powers that be. And if that happens..." He turned and pointed a hard bony finger menacingly toward the dense layer of ground fog that lay in the distance beyond the swamp, "they'll ship your ass off to work on The Wall!" With an emphatic snap of his wrist, he abruptly spun on his heel and stalked off to his machine.

Harry watched silently as the hairy man climbed aboard and

started noisily off down the mountain in a cloud of dust, dragging his log behind him on a short length of chain.

***

CHAPTER FIVE

"The wall, the Monday War, and General Havoc"

It took Harry three days and three nights to cross the desert, skirt the town, and finally reach the fuel depot that lay at the very edge of the swamp. He was hungry. Huddling in the darkness behind the stark white building, he observed a truck pull in and stop beneath the bright overhead lights. It was a large truck designed to carry livestock. The finish was very rough and in the rear, long wooden slats ran high in the air. He crept closer. Between the slats, he could see the naked bodies of human beings stacked like pieces of firewood, their starved, half-mad faces peering listlessly out through dull, unseeing eyes.

The driver of the vehicle climbed down from his position and disappeared into the innards of the station. He was a huge, bearded man dressed from head to toe in black animal skins. He returned a few minutes later with two other men. One pushed a large metal box on wheels, while the third carried a bright light which he began to direct in and around the mammoth truck. The driver walked behind and carried a long metal tube. Wherever the light would point up a sick or sleeping man, the leather-clad driver would insert the rod and there would be a short crisp buzz followed by a scream. When all the men in the truck were awake and screaming, the one with the metal box on wheels reached inside his container and pulled out large pieces of hot, steaming meat which he quickly stuffed between the long slats. When all three keepers were busy on the far side of the truck, Harry shot forward, quick as a lizard, and dipping in both hands, grabbed three chunks of the hot, steaming animal flesh and slipped back in the enclosing darkness.

He sat crouched, chewing on the tough gristly meat and reviewing what he had witnessed on his trek to the fuel station. He particularly regretted the roving dogs that circulated around the perimeter of the Happy Valley housing development. He would have liked to have gotten a closer look at the colored houses.

As he finished his meal, the giant truck departed only to be replaced by four even stranger vehicles. They were dull black in color and clattered as they rolled up on long metal belts which made shallow, jagged holes on the surface of the road. They were rectangular, and on the top a large spherical metal dome moved this way and that. From this protruded a long metal tube which served as an eye, and wherever the dome stopped, the tube came to rest and wherever the dome turned, so turned the long tube. Suddenly, the dome on the first vehicle tilted up and back, and from out of the machine crawled a tall, blonde woman. Soon the domes of the other three did likewise, and four women stood around smoking and laughing as the station man serviced their vehicles. When he was finished, he slapped his hand on the front of the lead vehicle and laughingly wished them good luck. The woman with the blonde hair responded by saying that luck had little or nothing to do with it; they all laughed as if sharing some great private joke.

Harry sat comfortably in the darkness, watching the strange vehicles depart and considered his possibilities. He sniffed the air. Winter was approaching and the swamp was on his left. His ultimate destination, as described by Desire, lay far to the East, beyond the swamp--beyond The Wall.

The sun was rising and he prepared to move, for to be discovered in such a place would be to become like all the others; this was a sacrifice that he was not prepared to make.

About a mile behind the fuel station he made a sad discovery. The swamp was wetter than he had suspected. While parts of it were relatively dry and supported dense clumps of marsh grass, by far the larger part of the swamp was a thick liquid, impossible to walk upon. Anxiously, he wandered back and forth at the edge of the swamp, his eyes keenly searching for a possible path out of Happy Valley.

As the sun drew higher his anxiety increased for he knew that at any moment he might be discovered and would soon find himself behind the boards of a truck bound for The Wall! Then there was a noise. He fell to the ground and looked to his left. From out of the early morning ground fog came a dog. It was a very large dog. And immediately behind it came another. Luckily for Harry the wind was blowing in his face and he had but their stench to contend with. They seemed distracted and gave him no notice, though they passed within ten feet of his body. This must be one of the Happy Valley dog patrols returning from their nocturnal excursion, he thought. Soon a continuous stream of the large, shaggy beasts were passing quite, close and though they noted his presence, they did not hesitate, but continued their loping gate back toward Happy Valley. He was relieved but confused by their behavior and then he noticed that in passing their stomachs almost brushed the ground. Obviously, they had so gorged themselves during some nocturnal orgy that they were barely able to trot.

As he lay in the warm, bubbling swamp muck, watching the wild dogs return home, an idea slowly formed in his mind. If their average weight was in excess of one hundred pounds and if they were indeed returning from across the swamp, then he had merely to retrace their steps and he would find a way out of this Happy Valley. He stood and began to run slowly against the direction of the dogs--out and over the swamp, through the fog in a wildly meandering zig-zag pattern. He was happily surprised to find that the path was much wider than expected. It was as if the dogs journeyed to their nightly feast en masse, first come, first served and then, once satiated, returned in single file. Gradually, as he moved out across the swamp the fog grew thicker while the dogs began to become fewer and fewer. Having no idea how wide the swamp might be, he anxiously increased his stride and began to run, for if he ran out of dogs before he ran out of swamp, he might be sure that when his hunger returned, so would the savage dogs of Happy Valley.

As the sun grew higher, the space between the dogs grew larger and larger. From time to time, he would have to stop and lay on the ground in order to detect a path through the fog and the mud, but then another straggler would suddenly appear and pass, to sleep off its gluttony by hearth and home.

As the sun reached mid-heaven, the fog began to burn off, and he first began to hear the terrible noise. The last dog had long passed with a prophetic growl and a fearful snap of its jaws that succeeded in sending him sliding across the foul smelling swamp muck on his stomach. From his position, he stared intently into the fog trying to ascertain the path. As he looked, the remaining fog began to retreat before his eyes. On the horizon, not a quarter mile way stood...The Wall.

The Wall stretched to the North and to the South around the perimeter of the forest of Content. It was roughly twelve feet high, six feet thick and stood exactly five miles from the banks of the river, Elin, which separated the forest of Content from everything else. It was essentially a defensive structure, initiated at the dawn of time by the Power That Was, to protect the populace of the forest from...Them. The labor force was conscripted from the society's criminal fringe; the political adversaries, artists, musicians, thieves and free thinkers. The Wall's physical construction was ingeniously determined by the terrain through which it moved. In rocky country, it was a stone wall; in forested areas, it was made of wood, and as it moved through arid terrain it became a brick wall. Five hundred yards off to the left of the wall, a large grandstand had been erected. The seating began twelve feet off the ground and soared another thirty feet above the wall. From there, the citizenry of Happy Valley could observe what it was the wall protected them from. Just the day before, five thousand Valley citizens had thrilled to the smoke and smell of a major tank battle taking place between The Wall and the river. Some observers were heard to complain that all the tanks looked the same, but then who could ever really distinguish one tank from another over a twelve foot wall in the midst of a battle taking place three miles distant. Suffice to say that the five thousand returned to their homes and spread the word that the enemy was close, in fact they had crossed the river. Thus additional funds were requested and approved, and the maintenance of The Wall was stepped up.

As the fog cleared, Harry saw a path and sprinted the remaining distance half crouched, half stumbling. He threw himself beneath the wheels of a long abandoned machine rusting at the very edge of the swamp. Luckily for him the brick making machine that he crouched under was long abandoned; the machine next to it was not, and the loud noise it created was grating on his nerves.

Poised like some huge, black pterodactyl at the edge of a primordial pool, it sucked up the wet swamp ooze through one end and noisily spit out crudely formed bricks from the other. Though some of the objects resembled bricks, most appeared to be chunks of fossilized excrement, and it was with this that they repaired the crumbling wall. It was a sad sight that Harry looked upon that day. Small groups of half-mad, starved, naked men standing nervously beneath the beast's quivering anus, anxiously awaiting the next load of bricks which they had to immediately sort and separate. If they lagged in their appointed duty, the numerous overseers, dressed in long, black, leather mourning coats graciously offered instant motivation. The impetus was delivered like the crack of a shot through the body of a six foot black swamp snake whip. If the laggard persisted, the next load of brick would, as often as not, crash down upon his head and mash him into mortar. And so it went, up and down The Wall.

The sorted bricks were moved to The Wall in the callused hands of runners. Each runner would carry two bricks, little packages of earth, to be pasted into a flaw in The Wall. While some runners had to travel over two miles, others had to travel but a few feet. As often as not, the runners were relatives of the overseers. Once bricks reached the flawed section of the crumbling wall, they were handed over to one of the many brick layers who would then paste them in place with a small daub of mortar. Since none of the workers were permitted to peer over The Wall, there was no scaffolding. Instead the taller men worked on the lower sections while the shorter men stood upon one another's shoulders to reach the upper portions. All the while, the black coated overseers would lash the workers mercilessly with their whips and scream incessantly, "*DON'T LOOK! DON'T LOOK*!" For in truth, if they looked, they would see that is was only a Monday war. But in the long run, it made little difference since no one ever returned from The Wall alive--not even the overseers.

That is, it made little difference, except to Harry. He had remained crouched beneath the abandoned brick-making machine awaiting his chance to dart across the open area and through a savage dog-sized hole that lay directly within his line of sight. He listened to the harsh explosive sounds of the brick-making machine and mingling with it, in the distance, beyond the wall, a yet unidentified "rat-tat-ta-ta-tat. KA-BOOM!"

Suddenly, an overseer pointed to the dog-sized opening and motioned to a couple of wall workers. The two runners approached to confer with the overseer and then jogged off towards the waiting pile of bricks. Without a reflective thought, Harry jumped to his feet and began sprinting hard, gathering speed, blocking out all thoughts but one. The two runners, who had just gathered their bricks immediately dropped them in astonishment. The poor naked men on the sorting pile looked up and grinned. Unfortunately, the huge brick- making machine did not grin, nor even hesitate in smashing them into a very poor grade of mortar.

Harry was halfway to his goal when he looked up for the first time and saw a dark-coated overseer closing quickly from the left. The overseer made an error by attempting to get between Harry and The Wall before raising his whip into strike position. For one unaccustomed to body contact sports, Harry exhibited a natural talent, lifting his arm at the wrist and then bending it at the last moment, so that the elbow neatly slammed into the overseer's jaw, lifting him off the ground and carrying him backward into the residual muck and festering swamp goo that gathered in large puddles in front of The Wall. Immediately, a loud cheer went up from the prisoners. This undoubtedly saved Harry's life, for the majority of overseers were thus forced to hold their ground, fearing a full scale mutiny.

When the siren went off, only two guards remained close enough to do Harry any damage. One, having seen his partner's mistake, drew back his whip, preparing to trip Harry as He sped past. Harry abruptly changed direction and succeeded in drawing the guard's whip. The remaining overseer, who had stationed himself in front of the hole, was more than a little agitated as he observed Harry closing and still gathering speed. He was intimidated by his size and general state of health for Harry was no docile, half-starved wall worker. At the last instant, the man in front of the hole tried to enlist the aid of two brick layers who stood at his side, but they just laughed. Recognizing the futility of his position, the guard hastily stepped aside as Harry flew past and dove neatly through the savage-dog sized hole.

The opening in The Wall was wide, but shallow, so that as Harry dove into it, he had to crawl out. He wished to remain optimistic, but when he finally raised himself to his knees and saw the black, one-eyed machine from the fuel depot looking directly at him, he I considered turning back to take his chances on The Wall. But then the turret lifted and a human voice cried out "QUICK--IN HERE!"

Harry crawled onboard the strange machine. He then quickly slid down inside through the open turret as the vehicle neatly swiveled and started off at a brisk pace across the burned off battle field scattered with rusting war machines and bleached bones.

Seated at the controls was an old gentleman with a long, drooping white moustache. He was dressed in summer khakis and wore a campaign hat with two bold strokes of embroidered lightening and five small golden stars clustered towards one side.

"Damned fine work, my boy! Two more seconds and they would have had you for sure!"

Harry had a hard time hearing the man's words over the rather loud music that blasted from the interior speakers.

"What's that you say? I can't hear you. I say, I'm afraid I cannot understand what you say."

"Eh? What's that you say--'hear you?' Of course I can hear you...oh, yes, of course." said the general finally turning down the sounds.

"My theme music, only music I ever listen to any more; gives me STRENGTH! I say, you made this old commander's heart proud. Two more seconds, just two more and they would have pounded your young ass into piss poor mortar!"

After pausing to catch his breath, Harry sincerely thanked his rescuer and the inquired who he was and what this thing, was that they were riding in.

"RISK! I love it! Makes the whole bloody thing worthwhile. My name? Havoc's the name son, General Havoc. War's my game and this fine creation you are riding in is a machine of *DEATH*! It's pure and only purpose is to facilitate one person killing another. I mean, what is it we have all come here for, if not to dance with *DEATH*?"

The general paused as if to reflect upon this sudden realization and then continued in a rather subdued tone. "A sort of quiet, lyrical beauty in that, if you've the sort of mind to ah...drink it in. And so, speaking of drink, you must have worked up a hearty thirst, bucking your way like that through the enemy lines. Say...you are one of them, aren't you?"

Harry hesitated, not quite knowing how to respond. Finally out of fear, he nodded his head almost imperceptibly as the general handed him a beer.

"Well..." said the general, dismissing the question with a wave of his hand. "Makes no damn difference to me who you are! Anybody, and I say again ANYBODY with balls enough to break away and take his chances crossing the battle zone to the river is a friend of mine!" The general raised his can of beer in salute and Harry did the same.

"So, you say there's a war going on here?"

"A war?" The general looked around skeptically. "Damn right, there's a war going on here--every Monday between dawn and dusk."

"But, why is the war only on Mondays? Strangest war I've ever heard of."

"Aye, and it is a strange war. I'm a bit embarrassed at the low level to which the once noble game of war has fallen. It's getting so you have to resort to all variety of subterfuge just to field a single team. Two teams? Well, you can just forget it! Impossible. Why, I've been running the war here for almost twenty years with just one side and it's not as easy as it may sound, not if you want to keep it exciting and keep the morale high."

Harry must have looked confused, "How can you have a war with only one side?"

The general smiled, "Unmarked tanks and no survivors. That's the secret."

Harry took a deep pull on his beer and eyed this general warily.

"Depressing, depressing. The only thing that keeps me going is the hope that the noise may one day attract a suitable enemy. That's why I keep the loud-speakers blaring out the sounds of W.W. VII night and day. Now there was a WAR you could sink your teeth into!"

"How long ago was that, General?" Harry peered out through a slit in the side of the machine. The surrounding terrain was a stark, contrasting study in black and white. Smoke was rising from the many small fires, with blackened patches of ground and human skeletal remains evident in all directions.

The old warrior tilted his head back and tried to remember. "It will come to me..." He wrinkled his brow. "Damnit, I can't seem to remember!"

Harry sipped his beer and watched the old warrior struggle with his memory. In spite of the general's obsession with death, it felt comfortable cruising inside the great machine with the music playing softly in the background. Harry tried to think of something pleasant to say.

"How did you ever become a general, General?"

Havoc glanced at him. "Not a general, son--The General! I'm the only one there is. It was a long time ago...let me think. It was a long, long time ago..." He continued to glare at Harry as if holding him responsible for his inability to remember.

"Oh yes, I remember, it was my brother." The general's voice began to take on a certain glow. "You see, at that time, long ago, my brother, Civil Strife, was in power. He was the *Power that Was*, as we used to say, and he was concerned because *The Wall* was not deteriorating fast enough to keep a criminal labor force even minimally busy. Well, this was cause for drastic action! He considered cutting back on the number of arrests. He even instituted a plan whereby the spouses of the women, who fought and were killed in The War, would receive healthy pensions. He figured that would make the men happy and thereby reduce the criminal element...boy, was he wrong."

"Pardon me, general, but what does the number of women killed in the war have to do with the laborers working on The Wall?"

"Ah ha!" exclaimed the General excitedly, slapping the firing mechanism of his largest gun with a loud explosive report and sending a twenty pound steel shell off over the horizon. "You are one of them!" he said with a suppressed chuckle. "I thought so. You see, the labor force was stocked with criminals and the only criminals left were the ones we called *political adversaries* or individuals who have harbored a deep and abiding dislike for the *Power That Was*. We called them *'P.A's'*.

"Only, nobody in those days harbored any deep feeling about anything except the husbands of the bored wives who were always running off to join the Army. So my brother, Civil, came up with the idea of granting generous pensions to the spouses of those killed in action defending their country. But of course, according to the law, any man refusing a pension would have to be carted off to The Wall as a political adversary." The general took a pause to open another beer and then, smiling, continued on, obviously delighted to have an audience. "Pretty clever, eh? Give pensions to the potential criminals thereby cutting back on the prison labor force. Pretty clever, only it didn't work! Backfired in fact. You see, the men were no longer about to fight and die in a senseless pseudo war; that had been a female prerogative for many, many years, but they were still a little ashamed and embarrassed when the little woman was brought home in a box.

"Most were so depressed, in fact, that they refused the generous pensions. You see, his plan only increased the prison labor force. So, he came to me smiling one day and says, 'Havoc, how do you propose to solve the problem of too many laborers on The Wall?' 'Well, Civil,' said I, 'the problem is a simple one. *Widen the wall.*' And so **The Wall** was widened from three feet to six and I was made The General of Happy Valley's all female self-defense forces."

The General smiled contentedly, congratulating himself on a once-remembered job well done.

Harry was still a little confused, but then he was a novice in the ways of man. "By that one suggestion you became The General?"

The General nodded. "But, of course, you must realize, son, you do not get to become a general or even The General based on what you do. No sir! It all depends on what you know." The old man tapped his bird-like cranium in a knowledgeable fashion. "Always remember, son, knowledge is power and knowledge shared with the right people is control."

"But your brother was the Power that was. Didn't that have

anything to do with it?"

"Well...that too," said the general, a little embarrassed. "But tell me, son, where are you headed? I can't rightly haul your ass around the rest of your days in this tank. Much as I might like to."

As the old man gazed at him affectionately, Harry told him about his plans to cross the jungle which lay on the far side of the river and eventually reach the Big Sea. The old man's eyes grew larger and larger as he listened to Harry's plans with increasing interest. Finally, General Havoc got so excited, he momentarily lost control of the tank and, in attempting to regain it, he touched off two rockets and 2500 hundred rounds of machine gun fire.

"***The Big Sea***, you say? Damn, now that's an idea a man can get his teeth into! If I were twenty years younger, I'd just desert my post and go with you. Yes, siree! ***The Big Sea!***"

The General then considered fording the river in his aquatic general's tank, but Harry pointed out that there might be a shortage of fueling stations on the other side. General Havoc found this hard, if not impossible, to believe.

"No," he said incredulously, "they're everywhere! They're EVERYWHERE! Aren't they? But, you're right, of course. I'm getting too old; only hold you up. Besides, I'm firmly entrenched here baby-sitting a sick society full of pansies and retarded children. With my brother gone, it would all fall apart like a wet cigar if it weren't for the few remaining responsible adults like my own self."

Harry calmly agreed and then, as he climbed out of the turret and prepared to jump down onto the smoking sand, he looked back and gently inquired why nobody ever tried to escape from their painful confinement on *The Wall*.

"Oh," said the old warrior somewhat distracted, "some do, but very rarely and most that try quickly get run down by an irate housewife. Seems that most people, given half a chance, would prefer to live in Hell itself rather than take a chance with the unknown."

"Why do you suppose that is?"

The general paused awhile before he slowly answered, "Well, I don't really know. I guess because there's always the outside chance that the unknown might turn out to be worse."

The lonely old commander of **The Monday War** let Harry off about a mile from the edge of the River Elin, with two canisters of beer, a blood sausage and cheese sandwich, and a prophetic bit of advice.

"Never forget the dream, son, and always remember, if you can't keep it afloat, at least keep it wet."

And with that, Happy Valley's only general fired a few more rounds across the river in another futile attempt to attract the attention of a suitable enemy and then disappeared back across the burned off battle field, hurriedly, like some strange hard-shelled desert creature scurrying towards it lair to avoid the heat of the noonday sun.

***

CHAPTER SIX

"Random Cause"
Part One

By the time Harry reached the bank of the Elin river, the sun had set over the water. He ate half of his sandwich, drank one can of beer, and fell asleep in the sand. As his eyelids closed, he sensed a dim light on the far horizon, followed by a series of high-pitched squeals. As if battling a physical pain, he tightened the muscles in his stomach and tried to push up through the beaded web-like unreality of dream sleep. But it was no use. Soon, as the light grew brighter, he began to feel the dizzy rumble of deep sleep approaching like a fast freight train....

He stood naked in a clearing surrounded by gigantic stones. By his side were the pale steel rails, gleaming in the moonlight. There were many people standing about, wearing strange costumes. He couldn't recognize specific individuals because their faces were obscured. Perched directly in front of him on top of the largest stone, sat a dignified gentleman in long purple robes. To his left, the large group slowly arranged themselves in rows, as if in a chorus, or jury. To his right, stood a grey-robed man whose facial expression had become permanently bent, creased into a dazzling display of frustrated rage.

The grey man dramatically withdrew a sheaf of documents from the folds of his robe and began to read.

"I am speaking to you, love, from the essence of what's true, love. Infinity was yours, laid before you. You had feet as a base from which to view the infinite, as it spread before you in all directions with you as the center. It was made meaningful by desire, and relevant through the freedom of choice. You had eyes from which to reflect love to all things. You had imagination as your crystal and you had an ego in which to hold it. You had, only by trusting, eternal realization, but chose instead limited recognition and labeled it time, mine, and knowledge! The graceful freedom to select and derive pleasure from the realization of selection has become a curse. You have all become fragmenters of The Dream!"
He looked up and glared directly at Harry, "Is it true that these words were spoken by you in the *Land of Was*, during the days of future past, before the flood that is yet to be?"

Harry looked around at all the strange people so intent upon accusing him of these words. It seemed that he was the defendant in some sort of trial.

"But, I'm not sure," he replied. "I mean anything is possible; but you see, I have never been to the *Land of Was*, during the *Days of Future Past*."

"Oh sure, we've all heard that before. But the fact that remains is the injunction against mankind that I have just read. Is this a probable utterance that you might have made, had you found yourself in such a place and of such a mind?"

Harry had to laugh, "This time is a tea-room, my friends, that I have quite consciously chosen to enter. You see, I am a vagabond, a gypsy, of sorts, and this time, my leaves spread before me...my fortune to tell."

"Oh, sure. Enough, jackass! Enough, and too much, I fear," said the grey-flanneled man. "Extend your right one to *The Book* and swear publicly!"

The angry prosecutor suddenly withdrew a heavy, black volume from beneath his long, grey robes and placed it in front of Harry.

"Swear by it!"

"Certainly", Harry replied.

As he touched the dry, dusty leather cover, everyone present immediately became as transparent as glass. Everyone, that is, but Harry and a tall slender stranger he felt standing in the distance directly behind him.

In the distance, he could hear the muffled sounds of war and though he suspected it was all merely a dream within a dream of little consequence, he could not ignore the manic actions of the prosecutor, nor the frantic posturing of the judge and jury suddenly struck dumb, but continuing to mouth their lines like transparent glass dolls on a small holiday stage. He felt like a man caught in a stream of anxiety swimming against the current, being swept along by the tide. Somehow there had been a misunderstanding. The stranger knew. It was all just a misunderstanding betwixt a group of misunderstoodlings caught at an intersection of easily misunderstandable assumptions. The stranger would know...

As the stranger touched Harry's shoulder he turned a corner in sleep and stumbled into waking consciousness. "I'm just a misunderstoodling!" He said, opening his eyes and looking wildly about. "You know, you were there!"

The stranger leaned closer and wiped the sweat from his brow .

"Where is there?" he said with calm, theatrical precision.

Harry sat up and looked around.

"I'm glad to see that you are well," the stranger continued, "I thought perhaps you might be very ill or wounded. You've been asleep for three days."

Harry looked around at the strange landscape, sandy and barren, except for isolated outcroppings of rock, a few stands of scrub trees, and, in the distance, the river. His face was sore and his body was covered with wind-blown sand. By his side was a can of hot beer and the rancid remains of a sandwich.

"For three days?" he asked.

"Yes," nodded the stranger. "For three days I have kept watch over you."

Harry lay back in the sand and moaned, "I'll just go back to sleep, if it's alright with you. I should be home in bed, you see. I really don't belong here."

The tall stranger laughed happily and clapped his hands together as if in appreciation of a great joke. It was then that Harry noticed that they were both approximately the same age. When the young man finished his melodic laugh, he leaned over and inquired gently. "Where is home, my friend?"

Harry started to answer and then discovered that his mind was blank. "Home...home..." he repeated the word as if searching for hidden meaning. It had a strange foreign and exotic flavor to it.

"Well then," the stranger continued, "do you know where you are now?"

"Well," Harry replied rather hesitantly, "within limits."

The stranger laughed again in his graceful way and clasped his hands together. "But of course you know where you are...going," he said.

"Oh yes!" Harry replied directly. "I am going over...there." And he pointed across the river.

The stranger smiled a rather enigmatic smile. "Me, too," he said after a moments hesitation. "Perhaps we can travel together?"

Harry nodded, "Yes. That would be fine."

The stranger smiled again and extended his hand. Harry grasped it and rose to his feet. "Good. Then it is settled. My name is *Random Cause*."

Harry stood rather shakily after his three day sleep, grasping Random's hand. "My name is Harry, glad to meet you."

Random smiled and motioned towards the nametag still pinned to Harry's chest. "Yes, I know. But come, you must be hungry. Let us ask the river for a fish."

As Harry stood and watched, Random waded into the river and began to purr like a summer wind passing through a grove of willows. Suddenly his arms leapt out of the water and in each hand he held a fish--brightly colored and flashing like drops of liquid sun.

He fried them on sticks over a small fire. Harry marveled at his new friend's skill and grace. Random wore nothing but a pair of white shorts spun from the fiber of the hemp plant, and yet, from his pockets he pulled an unending variety of useful items: flint for fire, salt for seasoning, a knife for cutting and trimming. Harry so admired his companion's skills that when he was finally offered a stick of chewing gum, he was not astonished.

For the next few days they played at being young. The sun was warm and the water was clear. Harry learned a lot from his friend, Random Cause. Harry learned how to fish and how to tell which green growing things were good to eat and which were poisonous. He learned how to find crayfish in the shallows and turtle eggs in the sand.

Each night they would sleep huddled around a small campfire at the water's edge and each day they would journey along the gently sloping shore at a leisurely pace, trying to determine a way across the river Elin. As the days passed one into the other, Harry continued to learn; one of the things he learned was that Random was very secretive about his past. Finally one day, Harry asked him where he lived.

"I live where I am, as I was trained," he replied simply enough. "And here I am, so here I live..." he motioned with his hand toward his head and smiled, "in this little ship that houses my mind, which is the source from which all things come, take shape, and give off funny smells." They both laughed.

Later, in the night, seated around a small fire at the water's edge, Harry stared at the phosphorescent waves breaking gently upon the shore and indirectly asked the same question again.

"Where do you sleep, Random?"

Without a moment's hesitation, Random replied, "I sleep on the tideline with my head pointed towards my direction of travel. I sleep with the glow-in-the-dark waves on my left, the burned-off battle field of reality on my right and the stars straight ahead, above me, held in place by *The Dreamer of All That Is*."

In the morning, when Harry awoke, Random Cause was gone. Harry followed a trail of footprints that bordered the river for about five miles until they veered sharply to the left, through blackberry bushes and over a small grassy hill. The trail continued through the sand, between two steep dunes and eventually led directly to the door of a substantial-looking stone house almost totally buried by the blowing sand.

Harry tried the door; it was open. He entered cautiously and slowly looked around. The house was relatively small. It consisted of one twenty-by-twenty foot room, crammed to the rafters with furniture and strange objects of obvious symbolic significance. The room was quite dark after the brightness of the morning sun. There were no windows; the only illumination came from the open door and the two small oil lamps held by two larger-than-life statues that stood by each side of the large door like ancient centurions frozen in time. There were intricately carved chairs and a long, golden lounge; behind that were two large wooden wheels leaning against a wall. Stretched across the ceiling was a beautifully-detailed painting of a woman with her arms spread as if embracing the universe. Situated in the very center of the room, directly beneath the painting, was a large piece of white stone, carved in the likeness of a sleeping man with his hands folded across his chest.

"That's my father," said Random's voice in the darkness. Harry jumped at the suddenness of the noise. In the shadows he could discern a hammock slowly swaying. "Random, is that you?" he asked hesitantly.

The man in the hammock lit another small lamp and placed it on a table beside him. Harry stared at the man who resembled

Random Cause but looked like a much older brother.

"Where is Random?" Harry asked.

"I am Random Cause," came the reply.

"But...you look so much older."

Random peered at Harry across the room with a steady gaze as if looking at himself in a mirror across the great pond of time.

"It's an illusion," he finally said. "I have more years today so in your eyes I appear to be older."

Harry didn't understand. "But...whose house is this?"

Random unfolded himself from the gently swaying hammock and began to stand.

"This is my house. This is, in fact, the place in which I was born, though not the place in which I will be finally laid to rest."

Harry looked at Random quizzically, dumbfounded by the sudden series of apparent contradictions.

"This is the land of my people," he continued, leading Harry to the open door. "My father's father's father is buried not ten miles from here." He pointed through the swirling sand toward the northeast where Harry saw, far in the distance, a pyramid of awesome proportions growing out of the desert floor like the tip of a partially exposed crystal.

"But, yesterday, I thought..."

Random silenced him with a wave of his hand.

"Those were but yesterday's thoughts and yesterday's thoughts are just practice for today."

He retreated again, back into the coolness of the dark stone house and reclined into the blackness of the hammock.

Harry watched Random's movements and then sat on a small, carved wooden stool across from him, obviously agitated. After some silence, Random inquired whether he had anything to smoke.

"No, I'm sorry," he replied without thinking.

Random turned in his hammock and shot Harry a piercing glance.

"Can't you offer a little...hope to a fellow traveler?"

Slightly embarrassed, Harry pulled the embroidered pouch from beneath his shirt. Removing the small pipe, he stuffed it with the smoking mixture and handed it over to Random Cause.

"I'm sorry, I completely forgot."

Random nodded and accepted the pipe.

"Tell me about your journey, my friend, from the beginning," he said.

Harry began to tell him about his journey and his encounter with the Geni of Desire and of the different stages of the journey as outlined by Desire and what would happen should he fail at any stage along the way. He spoke of the woodchopper and the savage dogs and The Wall. He spoke of everything, except the small clear capsule given him by Desire.

The pipe was passed back and forth as Harry spoke. He was happy to have someone to speak with about these things and Random was a polite and attentive listener, swaying gracefully back and forth in his hammock, never interrupting, never letting his gaze leave Harry's face. And then, when Harry finished his tale, Random slowly examined the small pipe as if for the first time and said in a low whisper, "That's a nice story."

Harry wasn't sure if he liked the inflection of his companion's comment.

"It is much more than *'a story'*," he said.

Random motioned with his hand as if to dismiss his concern.

"A story is simply the tale of a person on his way to a desired goal. It matters little if he even succeeds in reaching his intended goal, nor whether his goal be reality, or a dream..."

"It matters to me," Harry said. "It is my quest!"

"Yes," replied Random with a slow smile, "the quest--full of soft possibility and rising expectation." He handed the pipe back to Harry. "I once had a great uncle who went on a quest such as yours. He was my grandfather's brother, but it is getting late and you are in need of your rest. We will continue this at a later time. Here," said Random, rising from his place of rest. "You may sleep here in this ancient hammock of pleasant dreams."

Harry began to protest. He felt that he should continue with his journey, but it was late, and his head was heavy with sleep. So, like a wealthy person on holiday, he decided to spend another day.

In the morning, after tea and biscuits, Random resumed the tale about his great uncle who made it to *The Big Sea* and discovered, *The Children of The Sea.*

"But the *Geni of Desire* made no mention of *The Children of The Sea*?"

"No, I'm sure he didn't," responded Random mysteriously. "You see, these are no earthbound sailors; no mere fishermen nor kayakers! Nor are these questors, like your own self, who have given up the past and earthly reference points like fame and gain-games in order to pursue a *Higher Order*. No, these, who my great uncle discovered, are the wind sailors who know no land. These individuals spend their entire time amidst the ebb and flow of the tides. They ride the ridges and scout the troughs of the sea as intently as any range rider from the old western days. Like electronic impulses skimming the very ridges and ripples of current found within the human brain, these are the very eyes and ears of *The Dreamer of All That Is*. Their function is to see what there is to see and to hear what there is to be heard. They literally eye and ear for The Dreamer, moving eternally over the pond of time--*Floaters, Darters* and *Skaters* upon the surface, the retina, the pupil, if you will, of God!

"The largest of these are the Floaters," he continued. "Their ships are white, bleached from the salt and sun, originally cast from the bones of the large ones, the leviathans of the deep. These vessels are so large and move with such rapidity over The Sea that they appear not to move at all. Even the smallest of The Floaters cover many acres and appear not unlike large farm houses firmly moored within the earth of a well plowed field. The largest of The Floaters are more vast than even the largest city ever to be found upon the earth."

Harry sipped his tea and watched this strange man warily.

"The smallest are The Darters which serve as the individual form of transportation for The Children of The Sea. These Darters are very small and extremely fast. They, often as not, link up in centipede-like sections, forming flexible multijointed string-like roadways between the large Floaters. Over these ribbons flow the endless procession of supplies which are necessary to maintain one of the large floating cities. But though the Floaters are the largest and the Darters the smallest, the Skaters are the ones that truly captured my great uncle's imagination, for they are the pirates of space and time skimming over the surface of The Sea on an invisible layer of what he referred to only as--*intent.*

Though these vessels look not unlike sailing ships of old, through some secret process, these swift surface sailors are able to skim at will over the largeness of the sea on an invisible layer."

"What do you mean by '*intent*'?"

"Well," replied Random. "It is not my word, but my great uncle's. As he related it to my grand father, who related it to my father, who related it to me. 'Intent' is a form of anti-gravity, if you will, certainly more focused than mere desire and more potent than just hope. Intent is a force to be reckoned with! And when coupled with the sunsails of the imagination, well, theirs are only the fastest, most maneuverable, most fantastic vehicles operating within this time/space frame. Although there is always the prospect that, at any instant, another, possibly superior, vehicle might just sort of 'POP' through! But so far this has just never, ever happened."

Harry watched Random with eyes grown large with interest. "And what do these amazing creatures look like?"

"Their sails are not of cotton, my friend. Nor of nylon, nor of any acrylic fabric woven or created upon the surface of this globe. Their sails are spun from the seeds of realization, and, as a result, they have no edges, as neither do their gloriously colorful caftans. Though they occupy relative space and move at a specific velocity, they have no edges and cannot be contained nor isolated within any specific frame. It seems that they move across a greater floor in time, to the beat of a drummer only rumored to exist within our rather limited hall of reference. They are each and every one, very dramatic in appearance. They are the freest of the free. They are the personal emissaries of The Dreamer and if not full blown dreamers themselves, they are certainly fully credentialed dream-reps. They are cosmic pirates who choose to gather not beneath the blackness of skull and cross-bones, but before an image of The Sun! The uniforms of those who crew the water Skaters are described by my great uncle as being diaphanous caftans of brilliant rainbow hues, sparkling beneath the sun and giving off streamers of flash and color as they turn here and there upon the high sea. They often form a moving picture--literally, skimming over the surface at terrific rates of speed, with their bleached white skeletal hulls and their misty blue sails of imagination, deriving their sustenance directly from The Dreamer. All the while, the smooth yellow hum of intent, looking for all the world like a yellow light, seems to perfectly fill the gap between the hulls of their ships and the surface of the universal pond.

"The crews themselves often give the initial impression of flowers, for with their brilliant robes and exquisite headdresses they look not unlike the individual petals of an elaborate tropical plant or feathers constituting the plumage of a very rare and exotic bird."

Random stood and moved to the far corner of the darkened room where he stoked the small fire.

"Continue," Harry said. "Tell me, where do these creatures come from?" Secretly he was beginning to wonder if Random Cause wasn't one of the many distractions the Geni had warned him about.

"Where do they come from?" asked Random, hesitating in order to remember, or create a reply.

"Well, according to my great uncle, the elder Water Skaters, the original ones, entered The Sea from the most northern points: from the very center of the earth. These were often seen by beings of lesser order as a spray of Northern light referred to historically as the Aurora Borealis. The other, younger ones, are now apparently produced in the usual manner."

Random returned across the room and handed Harry a hot steaming plate of fresh vegetables.

"They are able to bridge the gap, between imagination and matter. The essential difference, you see, between a Skater and you or me is that they aren't, while we still think that we are."

In the light of the oil lamp Harry observed that his companion had aged from eighteen to thirty over the last few days. "But what do they do?"

"What do they do?" Random looked positively insulted. "They do as they please, of course. They play. They have fun. Skaters are, at one and the same time, angels and celestial vampires. Their only purpose, if purpose is truly the term desired, is to play! They were created from ecstasy and then immediately set free. They are the butterflies of consciousness, the otters of the universe. They are the first residents of The Great Surround.

They fan the flame and soak up the sun. They are the fingers that center the clay upon the universal wheel...they are the *Children of The Sea*!"

Random watched Harry very closely as if to see if he was paying proper attention.

"Sometimes they are like soap bubbles in a sea of foam winking on and off, out and in. And yet at other times, they have the consistency of the purest glass, clear and dense. And though they operate within this gravitational field, they are free to create their own self-organizing rings of singularity--their own little spheres of influence. They are the lords and ladies of change, separated from us only by a very thin wall of light. And yet they are completely aware of our presence. When a Skater casually tosses his cape over his shoulders, he is not unaware that universes are conceived, mature and die...all in a twinkling! They constantly reach up and out in an intuitive understanding that at the same instant, The Dreamer is reaching down and within and in that realization there is a profound touching. Seemingly it makes all the difference, to them as well as to us, the last phantom bodies still bubbling in the stream. You see, we are not the first, nor the most advanced, Harry. We are the last and the rest of the universe is urging us on."

"How come your great uncle was so lucky?" Harry said, laying aside his empty plate.

"Lucky, what makes you say he was lucky?"

"Well," Harry replied, "how was it that he was able to see and become aware of these wonderful creatures, these forces of change, whereas the rest of us remain blind?"

Random laughed, "We have all made contact at one time or another, my friend. Surely even you have felt the pressure from the presence of a nearby Floater or seen the flash at the corner of your eye from a Skater or Darter whizzing by. We have all made contact many, many times, my friend, but we all, seemingly as if by prior agreement, refuse to see what there is to see or to hear what there is to be heard. Often, upon feeling the rush of a nearby Skater, one is suddenly seized by what is commonly called creative inspiration. Many a person has been driven to press pen to paper or paint to canvas under the guise of artistic inspiration, when in reality it is merely the passing of a couple of Skaters engaged in supraverbal banter which reverberates down through the lesser frequencies. These illumines are much sought after in certain esoteric circles. Such was the force that motivated my great uncle to leave the security of hearth and home. He initially set out upon the sea in hopes of securing the benefits of such a creative spiritual encounter."

"Your great uncle was very lucky."

Random looked puzzled, "No, my friend, he just liked to have fun. There is a difference. He had a great sense of humor. He was, at one and the same time, the punch line to the joke as well as the impulse to laughter. He, too, wished to be a shaper..."

Harry stared into the flickering oil lamp for a long while, considering the pictures that Random Cause had painted in front of his mind's eye with his deeply felt words. Harry wished to stay and hear more and yet he felt impelled to leave, to be on his own way.

"Oh no," said Random suddenly as if reading his mind, "you can't go yet! Surely you have enough time for a bowl of smoke? After all..." he said, gesturing towards the remains of the meal that he had prepared for him.

"Yes, of course. How rude of me." Harry packed the pipe and handed it to Random and then sat back and patiently waited for the next opportunity to leave and continue on his journey. In retelling what may or may not have been his great uncle's actual experience upon the high sea, Random became more and more animated and began to fall upon specifics that were quite obviously beyond Harry's realm of experience. But through his growing animation, Harry began to perceive new and fascinating aspects of Random Cause's personality. Without the distraction of content, it was rather like observing the performance of a talented poet reciting in a foreign tongue. Random stood, after handing Harry the pipe, and began to move gracefully about the dimly lit room as if in a trance, using grand expansive gestures like an actor on a stage performing for an unseen audience.

Slowly, through the beneficence of the stony vapors, Harry's initial anxieties began to dissipate and float upward with the smoke. Gradually, Random's monologue became terribly exotic and Harry smiled as individual words and phrases conjured up images from other times and places. Like long forgotten lyrics to a favorite song, these words took on special meanings.

Random stopped in mid-sentence and looked down at him as if surprised and embarrassed by his presence.

Harry looked back, drowsy eyed from the corridors of his own imaginings and said softly, "It's like a poem, isn't it?"

Random visibly relaxed. "Why yes!" he said emphatically. "The Quest. It is like a poem..." Random sank back upon a carved wooden chair in the shadows and began to speak of his personal experiences.

Harry tried to concentrate on his images, but he was very tired and significant spaces were elapsing between Random's individual words. Some of the spaces created by Harry's lapsed concentration were quite large. Some were large enough to stand in and hold an opinion. Some were large enough, it seemed to live in and grow old. Thus he found myself hang-gliding into the land of sleep on pastel thermals created by his companion's exotic imagery.

Three short hours later in the darkness and the black, Harry's eyes snapped open like hinged doors on metal springs. Nearby, in the shadow, he observed Random's sleeping form. He gently retrieved his pouch and pipe from the low table and slowly opened the large stone door. The wind had stopped blowing. Quickly he slipped across the ghostly dunes like a fleeting thought, intent on finding his own way across the river.

***

CHAPTER SEVEN

"Random Cause"
Part Two

Of the four major rivers that separate the awesome forest of Content from the dense jungle of the Imagination, the Elin was the largest. At its widest, it stretched over twenty-five miles before encountering another shore. The river ran from all the way in the North to all the way in the South and served as the Western boundary of the approximate square that constitutes the bulk and body of the forest.

Though he found himself at the narrowest part of the river, the current was much too strong to swim, and by the end of the day, he was unable to find any material with which to construct a raft. Beneath a full and trembling moon, the darkness of sleep finally settled upon a very sad and tired questor. But he rose with the sun and optimistically continued his search only to grow more and more depressed as the day wore on. By evening of the fourth day, sadness was in his heart, despair was in the air, and the whole world began to reek of sundown.

By dawn of the ninth day, he began to seriously question the beating of his own heart. As his mind began to throw up grotesque images, his mouth would form the taste and soon the smell of his increasing anxiety began to seep along the shore like an ever thickening haze, threatening to block out the light of his inner being. Strange thoughts came in his mind, disturbing thoughts like the curling edge of a dream which refused to lay flat. All night he lay awake considering his options. By morning, he was positive that his only remaining expectation was sure to be a slow death, and with his last few remaining threads of hope he tried to visualize the possibility coming swift and soon. To linger on in this parched outback would be a fate truly worse than death.

With his mind thus centered about the grisly imaginings of his own demise, he spent the morning hours aimlessly stumbling along the river shore in a generally southern direction. He shuffled one foot after the other, listlessly observing the isolated clumps of bulrushes, the outcroppings of large rock and the small smoothly polished stones scattered about. The encroaching expanse of white, hot sand gathered about him like a slow, evil thought radiating its intent. Woe is fear that comes, not as a spy in the night, but as a whole battalion, shrouding the sun at its height and making the day a grim and dismal place indeed.

Like an army of ants, his worries and nameless anxieties began to swarm over him constituting a steadily growing irritation that threatened to engulf and consume him. Blotting out the sun, his emotions began to construct their parapets across his mind until light itself was more a memory than a source of illumination. He could not control the defeat that he felt, that he inhaled through his living heart, any more than the earth can protest against the rising water after a hard rain. He believed in The Quest and now only its completion would complete him.

He fell. An imaginary predator lunged at his neck as he fought to rise. Another snapped at his rump. He jerked his head around to confront his new tormentor only to feel a stab of pain at his flank. He tried to get up. He could no longer see. Flies, like buckshot, pelted the raw opening wounds in his psyche as he went down again. He no longer noticed the pain. He no longer fought against the outside threat. He staggered and fell. He struggled and staggered and fell.

As the sun began to draw low on the fourteenth day, he decided to hang himself from the very next tree. Too weak to swim, he hoped the tree would appear before dark, for to die by one's own hand at night, would be a pitiful thing indeed.

As he passed beyond some large rocks, he spotted it--the tree. It was a tall, lovely, strong-looking tree and in his excitement to be rid of his burdensome envelope of flesh, he began to run. And as he drew closer, he began to run even faster, even as a man dying of thirst might run towards water or a man in love might run towards the object of his affection. As he ran, he laboriously unfastened his belt and held it forward as an offering of great worth. As he drew closer, his eyes seized the tree and his mind began to devour it, branch by branch and leaf by leaf. The trunk was strong and thick and grew out from the river's bank into many strong limbs, any of which would be more than suitable for a man to hang himself. And the leaves; never had he seen such a veritable forest of soft, fragrant green.

The ancient wooden ferry with its sails hanging slack, lay waiting by the shore of the river, not thirty feet from the trunk of the tree. The aging ferryman sat at the very edge of the boat with his great goat-like feet dangling in the clean, clear water watching the setting sun's last light spread out over the river.

Harry had began his climb up the trunk of the massive tree and was well on his way toward his final dangling place, when he noticed the boat. He wouldn't have noticed it at all, had it not been that in order to get a firm grasp, in order to place his foot correctly, so that his belt might be wrapped around the proper limb, he had to take one last look at the water. Quickly he averted his eyes. Even as the ferryman stood, turning in his direction, still he remained intend upon his depressing task.

Random Cause stood casually with his hands on his hips, looking up at Harry with a slight smile, his now fifty-year-old face thoroughly lined by time and the river and yet still open and compassionate.

"So old, so old..." was all Harry could say as he looked down upon his friend
.

The ferryman nodded and smiled, "You stand there with paradise in your eyes, counting the leaves upon a tree in the forest of Content and speak to me of age?"

Random turned and began to throw off the ship's lines in preparation to sail.

Harry suddenly fell to the sand like a piece of overripe fruit, leaving his belt hanging from the limb in the tree
.

Random extended his hand and a shattered young man crawled on board.

"Do not be so impatient to die, my young friend," said the old sailor, "the world will offer up many opportunities on its own."

As the old ship began to move slowly away from Content towards the Imagination, Harry squatted upon the cracked planking of the wooden deck and slowly rocked back and forth, staring at Random Cause.

"You are afraid now-and tired..." said Random finally. "You are afraid of me. You think me a god or a devil and you are embarrassed for yourself and the thing that I witnessed. But look" he said, pointing first ahead and then behind. "We have departed the forest and now we move through the darkness of the unknown across the abyss toward the jungle of Imagination."

He leaned closer to Harry and spoke slowly in hushed, gravelly tones. "These two extremes form a conceptual pole, which this small boat slides across. This conceptual pole balances on a very thin line of time which spans this gorge of fear...and you are the point of balance, my friend." He sat back and seemed to slump slightly. "I am just a man and what you see in me is but a projection of yourself. We are moving now into a totally different reality and in the coming reality, you will have to use your most subtle inner senses. You will have to become as aware of your inner self as it is already aware of you."

The rays from the emerging stars that whorled overhead helped Harry focus and reintegrate. His breathing gradually became steadier. He felt stupid, but grateful, and relieved. He had come quite close to doing a very dumb thing.

"But Random...I feel so ashamed."

Random silenced him with a short sweep of his hand.

"Your embarrassment, Harry, is vanity and while vanity may be a useful device in the forest of Content, it has no place within the jungle of Imagination. Reflect upon your recent source of embarrassment..."

The boat moved slowly. Random tied off the rudder to a post and stood. He walked through a small hatch to a cabin below and shortly returned wearing a white hooded robe to ward off the evening's chill. He handed Harry a similar cloak.

"Your recent attempt to take your life was but a conspiracy between you and your inner self, Harry. Why do you think you selected that specific tree behind that exact rock? Didn't you pass twenty such trees which would have been just as suitable to your purpose? As soon as I discovered your absence, I took my boat to that certain spot and waited for your arrival, for it was obvious what you were eventually going to do..."

"But I had no plan. I merely wished to escape. I was afraid that you were one of the distractions the Geni of Desire had warned me of!"

Random nodded and turned up his hood against the wind until it covered all but his deep-set eyes. As Harry stared into Random's face he could not remember if Random was a young man suddenly grown old and grey, or an old man that had somehow given the initial impression of youth.

"That is only partially true, Harry, for both of our inner selves were aware of the purpose behind our initial meeting.

Distractions are also opportunities and the boat was only a matter of time. After all, I am the ferryman, but you could not sail into the void until you somehow managed to conquer or discredit your essential vanity."

Harry sat for a very long while in silence, watching rust form on a wide iron band wrapped around the base of the mast of the ancient boat. Gradually, the water became as smooth as silk with no visible wind, and the ferry sat stationary in the darkness with sails slack. He listened to the creaking of the wood and felt totally and absolutely alone in the void; poised at the very edge of some perilous abyss.

Random hunched over and began coughing.

Harry glanced up, but his cough abruptly ceased.

"In another time and in another place," Random said, "I found myself in much the same position as you. And then, one day, while walking through the dense inner ring of Imagination, I made a startling discovery. As I passed by one of the many green, brackish memory pools that dot the landscape in that specific region, I happened to glance down and within the subtle reflection of my own eye I, discovered something quite miraculous! Suddenly the *'reality'* of it hit me and I began to roll on the ground, or inside myself, or perhaps the universe rolled while I, in my most innocent trust, witnessed the exact moment of transition--from winter to spring. Quite without warning, I found myself, like Narcissus, a captive of the pool."

"And then...what happened?"

"Well," said Random Cause, "I would still be a prisoner, had it not been for a storm that came along and stirred up the surface of the pool enough to eradicate my image. At the moment I was grateful, ecstatic, for the release and the relief. *Finally*,' I thought, 'I can continue my journey.' But the memory of the realizations I had found in the green pool kept pulling me back. I would get no further than a mile or so, when the pull of pure memory would draw me, like the moon draws the tide on the river Elin.

"But something had changed. It no longer held me, and yet it would not let me go. I would hover over the pool, watching my face and staring deep into the reflective mind for hours, and hours and yet--nothing! No realizations, no insights, no mighty earth movements!" Random hesitated to cough and clear his throat. "You see, it never was the pool, not really. What initially held me was the vision, the Mandala, the eye, of another...on the quest! Once I was no longer on the quest, the pool cut me loose."

Random coughed once again and then leaned over and looked directly into Harry's eyes.

He could feel the old man's hot breath on his face.

"Do you understand the meaning here?"

Harry swallowed and nodded.

Random sat back and tried to smile, "Good. And so..." he continued, looking away for the first time in a long while. "Since I could not progress any further through the dense jungle of the Imagination, after what I had realized, and since I could hardly return to the forest of Content, I became the ferryman at the causeway and swore to live out the remainder of my days half in Content and half in Imagination, hopefully to become the connection between the two. This ferry is now my prison, friend, and you are now--my pool..."

Harry felt sad recalling what Desire had said about those who were to become Shaman and markers. At that moment, a rending flash of light creased the sky and he glimpsed the other shore in the distance.

"Perhaps it is time for you to continue with the quest," Harry said. "Perhaps you are to go on with me..."

"No, no," he said, dismissing the idea as ridiculous. "I am just a sick old man now. Soon I will die. Besides, no two people can ever go on the same journey."

"Surely you are as young as you ever were?" Harry said. "You told me that age was only a projection. I see you! You are ageless. You are as young as you ever were. I have heard your words, Random, and they are the words of an adventurer on the quest!"

Random smiled slowly and gently clasped Harry's shoulder.

"That is because of you, Harry. For these past few days I have had the privilege of seeing it all again through the eyes of youth. I thank you for that."

He began to cough once more and at that moment, it began to rain; a drizzle at first, and then the wind rose from the North tightening the sails. "Here," he said, placing Harry's hand on the tiller, "...steer for the shore." And then he moved forward to trim the sails.

"But there is still time," Harry shouted into the wind.

Random returned from the bow and took the tiller. "No..." he said, "there is no time. Time is an illusion, possibly the *GRAND* illusion. It is a parade, my friend. It takes only as long to pass as it takes and you are, at one and the same time, the curbside observer, the drum major, the major-domo pompously standing high atop the reviewing stand and the last street sweeper to pick up the final bit of rubbish on the following day. It all happens at once."

He moved forward again as the old ferry neared the shore of Imagination and asked Harry to assist him with the lines. By the time, they had the ferry securely tied to the shore, the storm had increased in intensity and Random appeared to be quite ill. Harry succeeded in helping him to a small thatched hut not far from the shore. Inside, he found a small cache of food, a fire pit, and a straw bed. Random smiled feebly and asked to be put to rest.

Outside, the world grew quiet once again. The rain dripped listlessly, creating furrows in the earth. Inside, Harry kindled a fire and brewed some tea.

"Listen, my friend, things grow quiet once again," said the sick old man.

Harry nodded in agreement for the storm had indeed grown still. He brought the tea over to Random's pallet and set it down.

"Shush...listen to the sound of silence, Harry. Do you know what that is? It is *time* slipping through our fingers!"

Harry sat at his side and sipped the fragrant jungle herb tea.

By dawn, Random had grown weaker and had begun rambling on incoherently, speaking of himself in the third person. For the first time in days, Harry had succeeded in getting a good night's sleep. He looked forward to departing on his journey, but faced with Random's worsening condition, he could not force himself to leave, at least not until the old man regained some of his strength.

"He is hungry--" said Random in a pitiful whine, "a little nourishment and then with full belly he will die peacefully and quiet..."

Harry nodded at the old boatman and prepared porridge from oats and freshly picked blackberries that grew on the hut, but Random was not satisfied. He rejected Harry's efforts like the doting mother of the man instead of like the man himself.

"No! No!" he said, raising himself up from his bed on one elbow. "This will never do! He can not eat such things!" He looked up at Harry with an expression of utter disdain and turned the bowl of porridge upside down on the dirt floor. "These things are for animals, not for man! This man needs meat and strong coffee and then perhaps...something to smoke?"

Harry looked closely at Random, suspecting perhaps a game or another lesson, for though he did look old, frail and a little crazy, he did not look to be on the verge of death.

"Now, get him a fish!" said Random with the harsh brittle tone of command.

Yes, a fish, Harry thought. That could be done.

As he moved down the path to the river, he looked around and experienced a great joy. Until then, he had not fully realized that he was, in fact, at the very edge of the awesome jungle of Imagination. The light was clear and warm, but with a definite bluish cast and the fragrances that oozed from this wet, wild world were alarming to his senses. Yes, the jungle aura was spectacular and a bit ominous.

Kneeling at the water's edge, he quickly trapped a large green fish with small, darting orange eyes. Back inside the thatched hut, he fried it over the open fire on a stake.

"It smells so good, Harry. Yes, yes, you have done well. This is what he needs! See how he will eat it!"

As they began to eat, Harry put some coffee on the hot coals.

"How is he doing?" Harry inquired, humoring the old man.
"Oh," said Random, distracted by the process of digestion, "oh, quite well."

Harry leaned forward. "Good. I am so pleased for him. Tell him then, that I will be going soon. If there's anything further that he needs..."

"Oh my!" said Random suddenly sitting up. "You mustn't leave. You can't leave...not yet! He would surely die. We need you. He speaks very highly of you. Without you, he would have no reason to live!"

"Surely you exaggerate. He is, as you say, old and I might add, very wise, but we have only known one another for a few days."

"Seventeen days!" said Random sharply, "Seventeen days! You forget you slept for three days in the sand while I, I mean he, watched carefully over you."

"But, even so, " Harry said, "what could a person as young and inexperienced as myself possible be able to offer a man as wise and experienced as yourself?"

Random's eyes glowed over the coals as he saw that Harry refused to fall into his trap. "You owe me, Harry! I ferried you across the river. I saved your life *TWICE*! I fed you and gave you knowledge. You owe me something."

Harry looked at him. He was shaken by Random's intensity but not really surprised. Cagily, he asked, "What do I have that you could possibly want or need?"

The old man settled back on his bed of straw. "Let us not bicker, Harry. I am old and soon will die. I do not need anything except perhaps a friend and companion in my final hours."

Random's words were spoken with such sudden and honest emotion that Harry felt his defenses drop.

"I think I need medicine, Harry."

"All I have is my smoking mixture given to me by Desire; you're certainly welcome to that."

Random shook his head. "I'm afraid I need something stronger than that, Harry." He turned his head and wistfully gazed out the small window opening. The rain had stopped. He motioned with his hand for Harry to approach closer. He looked at the old man and moved to his side, for somewhere deep within he suspected that Random's cause was fair and just and he further suspected that one day, he might find myself in a similar position.

"The universe smiles on your passage, Harry. It is a generous universe. I feel sure you will reach your goal." He patted Harry on the arm and continued to stare out the window. "Please forgive me. I know I must appear ridiculous in your eyes. But forgive a sick old man for his craziness, for his old man's stench and uncommitted yearning."

He turned his deep dark eyes, that seemed somehow to focus on eternity, toward Harry and grasped his arm tightly.

"It is painful, my friend...waiting to die..."

Harry reached into his pouch and slowly withdrew his hand. In his palm rested the small, clear capsule given him by Desire. "Take this Random. It will make you well and strong again." he said.

Random retrieved the clear capsule from Harry's hand and quickly looked away. "You cause me to feel embarrassment, Harry..."

Harry cut him off with a short movement of his arm. "Your embarrassment is vanity, Random, and as I've heard tell, it has no place within the jungle of Imagination."

Random looked up at him and smiled for the first time in a long while.

"You have reflected well upon your recent source of embarrassment my friend. I am sorry, but I feel very tired now." He placed his right hand melodramatically over his heart. "I feel like the last gasp of a frail sparrow being slowly crushed beneath the evolutionary wheel of realization..."

Harry laughed, "Yeah, I hate it when that happens. Well, I think that you are well on your road to recovery." As he stood, he noticed that the clear capsule was no longer in Random's hand.

"You really don't have to go, you know..." he said. "This is a pleasant spot and there is still much I could tell you of places and time."

"Yes," Harry said. "But those are your places and your times. I must go now before it becomes dark again." He began to leave.

"But..." said Random Cause, slowly getting to his feet, "surely another day wouldn't..."

Harry turned in the doorway and interrupted him. "To me, it is no longer merely another day."

The old man gathered his long white robe around him and feebly followed Harry outside onto the path.

"So...my impetuous young friend, like two rafts approaching over a rough sea, the forces that drive us together eventually form the wash that precludes our touching..."

Harry appeared not to have heard, and continued down along the path into the jungle, smiling. Finally Random turned and began to make his own way back down the path toward his boat and the river.

They both silently walked the path in opposite directions, but eventually they turned for one last look; for in the final analysis, love is a duel. Random was now a youthful looking man again in clean white robes. Harry was not surprised, for what he saw was but a reflection of his innermost self. This was, after all, the *jungle of the Imagination*.

***

CHAPTER EIGHT

"The Imagination and the White Knight"

Harry turned away from the past (like an extraneous thought) and proceeded anxiously down the twisting overgrown path that constituted the entryway into the jungle. At once, the air began to feel heavy and as he descended deeper into the afternoon light, the sun was gradually devoured and swallowed by the ever-increasing lushness of the surrounding vegetation. This was in turn replaced by a bluer hue, generated in some way by the jungle itself. The very idea seemed to embrace him and it was dense, for his quest had finally led him to the jungle of Imagination where the seed of paradise is sown.

He moved on through thought and process, observing the miracle of pure visual phenomena in its myriad aspects, for in the jungle, the visionary becomes benevolently blind to all but the seedling paradise that is carried within, and nurtured through the silvered stalk of spine that connects the beast and the dreamer.

Continuing on through the lush humid greenery, he heard the sound of a stream and he approached the sound, for in his mind all streams led to rivers and all rivers led, eventually, to the sea. On his way toward the stream, Harry passed immense butterflies that undoubtedly lived forever and stained the air through which they passed with the lingering color of their being. Lightening bugs flashed every imaginable color, even during the blue neon brightness of the jungle day. As he pushed forward, he was seized by the unnaturally seductive aroma of such indescribable impact that it caused his nostrils to flair and his pulse to race. He quickly increased his stride, advancing aggressively through the restricting jungle of soft possibility and the tall stands of vibrant potential, only stopping from time to time to push aside one of the many creeper vines of tangled thought that threatened to strangle his mind with echoes of eternity.

What, he tried to imagine, could be the source of such an incredibly beautiful odor? And then he began to hear music, for he was in the jungle where crickets chirped their rhythms in different tones, while flocks of song birds circled high in the sky. It was luminous! Close by, large bullfrogs and swamp geese trumpeted their approval. In the clearing, a black flamingo danced proudly with a white swan, while rainbow-hued peacocks strutted their stuff through the surrounding forest.

"Is this paradise?" Harry wondered. As if in answer to his question, a grey wolf, the size of a saber-toothed tiger, roared from the dense undergrowth and tore into the white swan, ripping open its throat and dragging it back into the bush. As far as the black flamingo was concerned, nothing had happened--it continued to dance.

Instinctively, Harry crouched low, hugging the ground, attempting to make himself invisible. The air vibrated with the sound of flies come to share the grey wolf's feast. He felt many eyes upon him but finally, sensing he was in no danger, Harry stood and continued downhill toward the sound of the stream. And then he saw it, a purple, infrared stream running right through an imposing forest of immense incense trees. As he drew closer, his feet sank into the accumulated ash which dropped from the smoldering trees. Passing a stand of stout, red bamboo, he selected a strong dead tube to use as support and leisurely strode to the very edge of the stream.

The water, if indeed it was water, shimmered and pulsated. It seemed to refract light. From certain angles, it gave the appearance of a prism, with lines irradiant like spider webbing. Harry's eyes traced the course of the purple fluid and, in the far distance, high on a hill, he observed a large white rock formation from which the stream seemed to originate. As his eye traced the stream's path in the other direction, he saw still, green pools of varying diameters, bordering the stream as it ran into the dense jungle overgrowth.

Kneeling by the side of the stream, Harry passed his hand over its surface. The liquid trembled and slid between the vibrations of his passing hand. Its radiance had him entranced. Carefully, he lowered his left hand into the liquid and smelled it, and then, raising it to his lips, he touched it with his tongue. Much to his surprise, he discovered that it tasted and smelled exactly as he imagined it would.

Flush from inhaling the vapors of discovery, Harry's attention nimbly leaped across the small purple stream and seized upon the placid concept of a green stagnant pool situated near by. Standing upright, he cast his attention like a fisherman, so that he might better appreciate the character of this particular pool.

With his attention thus split--half on one side of the purple stream and half trolling across the surface of the stagnant pool--he found himself suddenly vulnerable, seduced and trapped like a hare in an open field. The initial realization was of an aural nature, a very low tone, produced perhaps by the smooth, slow stride of an exceptionally long snake or maybe it was merely the surging tone of a distant bridge. In any case, it was extremely base in origin and abruptly alerted the tiny fibers of Harry's inner ear.

Something was wrong. And then, as he helplessly watched, a tiny shadow touched the smooth green pool at its very center. It was a mere pinprick of black and in another place in time, it might have been conceived of as a pinprick in the surface of a small pillow of silken green perhaps and immediately dispatched to some neural outback of residual memory as an event of little or no significance. But in the dense inner ring of youth's imaginings, the soil was fecund and anxious for sudden change.

In less time than it takes to tell, the tiny spot of shadow abruptly spread like an unchecked virus towards the outer edge of a cell and the initial low tone began to rise in volume, as it slid up through the octaves resembling a steam locomotive about to explode.

Harry stood, a defendant in the dock, forced to passively witness a goodly portion of his attention about to be snatched away by an awesome bird of prey which apparently fed on stray conscious energy, as a hawk might feed on stray rodents. Stunned, indeed hypnotized by the immense implication of the idea, Harry felt like a young deer frozen in mid-stride beneath the powerful glare of an on-rushing automobile's headlights.

Hovering at point-balance, he thus savored the heady aroma of inevitability and watched as the giant predator descended. Its massive, fifteen foot, grey leather-like wings curled into its body like the leading edge of a tidal wave about to break upon the innocence of a kitten. Like the last closing millisecond of eternity, the sleek, grey winged beast closed with the surface of the small, green pond, its awesome claws extended, its shriek of intent now focused far beyond the realm of man. Gathering energy thus, the smoking body of the Phoenix shattered the still surface of the pond, and as it did, a goodly portion of youth's vision burst into flame. A small but relevant slice of Harry's conscious attention, once divided, was gone...forever.

Harry's body stood limply erect, his jaw slack. His once rather simple, well organized mind felt like it was running down his leg and gathering in a murky puddle at his feet. Suddenly his slack-jawed body snapped to attention like a fisherman's long neglected line hit by a large shark--and his inner eye observed the boiling pool of flame abruptly throw up the head of the bird. But now the once grey leather-like head of the large predator was gold. He blinked in disbelief and the image of the large bird's golden head retreated back into the broiling flame. Again-this time with the scream of a noontime factory whistle-the creature's head appeared, twisting and turning repeatedly trying to extricate itself from the flame. Harry watched in shock, his extraneous thoughts masked by the ultrasound of the beast's anguished longing to be free. Harry was left with but two alternatives; to believe or to disbelieve, to trust or to doubt.

As a sliver of doubt began to taint the innate purity of his belief, he witnessed the creature's strident effort collapse in an awesome shower of sparks! With his attention thus riveted, he watched in helpless astonishment as once again the thrashing beast began to emerge from the fiery pool. This time, though, as he observed the bird's golden head appear above the tops of the flame, the creature's intense effort bypassed his mind and touched his heart--thus the connection was made and immediately the longing for rebirth became as important to Harry as to the Phoenix! Harry now fervently lent his energy along with his attention, for the duality in his mind was at once unified and clarified by the passion of his heart. Soon, as his hope merged with the bird's desire, the entire project began to rise in the broiling flame, like an idea who's time has come. The bird's once steel grey wings now flashed gold in the neon blue of the imagination, giving off a crisp, electric brittle smell like lightning. As the Phoenix finally stretched its golden wings clear of the fire, the implication of the metamorphosis stirred in Harry's mind, and caused him to vacillate and become self-conscious once again. At that exact moment, one of the creature's wings suddenly dipped and then crumbled, causing the body to fold in descent. As the golden wing reentered the flame, Harry's mind was purged and unified as, this time he screamed out from the pain and effort and intense concentration required for creation. Yet, as the pain moved through his mind to his heart, it was instantly transformed into humility and awe, and at that exact moment he witnessed the Phoenix finally and resolutely take wing on its initial flight from the fiery pool of its own realization.

Once clear of its nest of flame, the massive bird stretched its golden wings beneath the sun, and rolling over slightly, turned a large dark eye toward Harry standing by the small infrared stream far below. As he stared up at the incredible product of the Imagination, the golden bird slowly opened its beak and shattered all remaining doubt and objectivity with a shriek so awesome that it caused Harry's knees to buckle and he collapsed. High overhead the golden bird circled, its dark, black eyes receding in the distance like twin black holes in deep space.

Harry remained where he lay, aware that he might, at any instant, be terminally distracted by the vanity of his indulgence. Yet he was fascinated by the actions of the long, slow thought, curling around in his mind painting pictures of a golden bird gracefully soaring through the neon blue. High above, the bird's cry filtered down to him as the distant trill of a peasant's wooden flute.

Harry gripped his pole of red bamboo for support and raised himself to his feet. He looked around as if for the first time. The surface of the green pool was again placid. He looked away. After a moment, he lifted his eyes and sure enough, there, high above in the distant beyond was the golden speck. Again he heard the soft trill of a wooden flute. He looked down at his staff.

"From this stick", he thought, "I shall create my instrument, a musical instrument, a navigational aide for future use."

And a splendid instrument it was, too, forged in the dense, fertile humus of pure imagination and tuned and tempered over the flame of eternal youth. It seemed an essentially intuitive process undertaken in the midst of a dream, within a dream. How it was done and to whom should go the final credit for craftsmanship is irrelevant. The emergent fact, and final realization, was a tubular section of red bamboo, hollowed and holed so as to produce with, but the merest wisp of human breath, a seemingly infinite variety of harmonic tones.

And so, Harry walked from beside the pool, strengthened and renewed, for he knew in his center that as he blew into the flute and gave that instrument its life and vitality, so the Dreamer of All That Is blew its intent through the fleshy fabric that constituted the instrument that was Harry. And so it is that life is often born and born again beside still, virgin ponds, untouched but for the mind of man and the breath of the Dreamer.

Harry rambled on day after day, observing the variety to be found within the imagination, and gaining proficiency with his instrument. On and on, deeper and deeper he progressed, generally following the path of the purple infrared stream--down into one enticing valley and up the other side, only to find yet another deeper than the one before. Finally he entered one steep valley that he sensed was somehow different. This particular valley scarcely looked at all like the jungle that he had become accustomed to. The trees were much larger and the spaces between them surprisingly clear of the customary jungle clutter. He stopped and listened patiently, but could not detect the slightest sound. The air was as still as a hunter. He carefully placed his flute in his belt and moved off in the direction of the stream. After walking an appropriate distance, to where the stream should have been, he stopped, puzzled. He looked toward the white cliff that was to have been his destination, but the valley was too deep and all he could see were rocks and trees rising above him in every direction like gigantic blades of grass. Harry tried to think rationally, to consider objectively but his mind felt like sand in an hour glass who's time was about to run out. He finally sat down on the forest floor and carefully laid his instrument in front of him. He was lost. Again.

"A point of focus..." he thought.

At that instant, a point of focus arrived in the form of a thin, black wooden shaft twenty-eight inches long. The shaft struck the ground immediately in front of him. The point of the shaft was embedded far into the soft humus of the Imagination and the long black feathers so carefully situated on the emerging end left no room for doubt. This was an arrow! He stared at the bizarre object as if it were a lethal viper. And then the ground began to tremble. Harry lifted his eyes from the arrow toward the sound and couldn't decide whether to cry or go blind.

Bearing down on him at an incredible rate of speed, was a large white horse. It was a magnificent, four-thousand-pound, hard-charging beast in full medieval battle dress; a 12th century war horse from the other world, its long white battle vestments dragging in the dust, creating veritable storm clouds of panic and confusion in Harry's young mind. Seated high atop the hard-charger was a most awesome looking creature covered from heat to foot with what appeared to be large, white metal scales. In one arm, it held a severely-pointed, twelve-foot lance. In the creature's other arm, it held small white shield and emblazoned across the front of the shield was a single red rose.

"This thing," Harry thought, "from out of some mythic child's nightmare, undoubtedly survives on the moist warm blood of questors such as myself and keeps creatures like the Phoenix as house pets."

His immediate response was to flee, but before his muscles could tense toward flight, the obvious futility of the gesture washed over him and he chose, instead, to close his eyes and think of something pleasant.

The creature pulled his mount to a halt immediately in front of Harry's stationary form and prodded him with the metal tip of his lance. Harry fell slowly over on his side and opened his eyes, positive that he was soon to be dead.

"Aye and 'tis glad I am that ye be still in one piece!" said the white knight, posting his lance in the ground and briskly flipping up his metal visor. "In the nick of time, I say. In another second he would 'ave skewered you like a bug on a pin!"

Harry could only stare wide-eyed at his apparent savior. He was intensely glad to see that it was a real flesh and blood person behind the ominous facade and not an evil creature at all.

"Say," said the knight, removing his weighty helmet and placing it over the pommel of his saddle, "you don't happen to have a flagon of rum do you? Or a skin of cool wine?"

Harry sat up and nodded helplessly. "Sorry," he said.

"'Tis just as well, I shouldn't really be drinking on the job anyway. But I can tell you, it sure is hot dusty work avenging evil and saving the distraught and the distracted. Say, how about some water?"

Harry shook his head and then pointed in the direction of the stream. "I've no water, but there is a stream..."

The white knight curled his lip in disdain. "Aye and there's eternity for anyone fool enough to drink from it! No young fellow, I'm not about to sip the brackish run-off from the caves of Nth Degree! Not while I'm still hale and hearty. I've my duty to pursue in the person of the villainous Black Knight!"

"But I've seen no black knight?"

"Aye," said the horseman, shifting in his saddle, "and you're not likely to, but..." and he pointed to the black shaft embedded in the ground. "It's obvious that he's had a look at you!"

Harry shivered at the thought of the arrow. "But where is he now?"

"Aye, and it's always hard to tell," said the white knight leaning forward in his saddle and looking around warily. "He hides in the overgrowth of the Imagination. He thrives in...the spaces..."

"The spaces?" Harry asked.

"Aye, lad," replied the knight with a stern look. "The spaces. The spaces between the rocks. The spaces between the trees, between objects, people, ideas...words! Look around you, he could be anywhere. He snatches up the unwary traveler and feeds him to his carnivorous steed, Chaos!"

Harry slipped his flute into his belt again and looked skeptically at his apparent savior.

"Aye, lad, I can see that you're a non-believer, but beware the lush silence that hovers in the spaces between, for Chaos is an awesome mount with a prodigious appetite and the Black Knight is but the ruthless servant of the evil beast!"

Harry nodded

"And who might you be?" said the knight. "And, if I might be so bold, what might be the nature of your mission?"

Harry hesitated, attempting to phrase an appropriate response.

"Well? Be quick about it, for I've got to be moving forward in pursuit while the evil varlet's trail is still warm!"

"Well," Harry said. "I'm on a quest to find *The Muse*. My name is Harry...and who might you be?"

The man in white armor laughed heartily. "Why, by all that's happy-go-lucky, you are a strange one. I should think it's perfectly obvious who I am! I'm the White Knight, doer of good deeds, savior of the poor and misbegotten, avenger of evil and bringer of glad tidings. And," said the knight, leaning forward in his saddle and whispering in low conspiratorial tones, "if it's truly the mews you're searching for, just follow in the direction I've come and you'll be on it in no time.

"But now," said the warrior, straightening in his saddle, "if you'll hand up the evil doer's villainous tool, I'll be on my way, 'fore this hour's time is past."

"But sir, what is your name? I mean, who are you and from where do you come?"

"Aye, my lord, you are full of silly questions for one so young. If it's a handle you're after, just say I am Sir Vain, The Avenger!"

"And where do you come from, Sir Vane?"

"I'm from the castle through the trees, just beyond the mews." Sir Vain snapped the metal visor low over his eyes.

"Please tell me something of the Muse, sir, for I've come a long way."

Sir Vain nodded his head sadly and raised his metal visor. "Forget the mews, lad, it's a low goal unworthy of one such as yourself, indeed more fit for beast than man. If it's a quest you're after, go find yourself a lady in distress. Now there's a quest most regal indeed, far more noble than a common mews!"

Before Harry could question him further, the white knight withdrew his lance from the soft earth and prepared to leave.

"Now I must go, so off with you, boy. Avanti, while thouest youthful thread is on the rise! Aye, and fear not sweet youth, for many a nervous needle hath been pierced by the stiff swiftness of a well thrust thread well taut."

With a lewd wink, Sir Vain dropped his visor and wheeled his horse to depart. "And don't forget, lad, if all else fails, many a glorious moment hath been spent with a well taught maiden fairly bought!" And with a lusty, "Har-har-har," he was gone, vanished through the trees and into the dense jungle beyond with a lightness and gentility that stood in contrast to his obvious mass.

As Sir Vain turned to leave, he waved his heavy gloved hand, and in that action, he appeared to become extremely light and airy. His weighty metal- clad fingers were suddenly like silver feathers cast from some high flyer, and as his armored body passed through the dense undergrowth, it parted the humid vapors, just so, like the whoosh of a butterfly's wing on the upward swing.

***

CHAPTER NINE

"And"

Part One

There it stood--imaginatively cloaked in dense jungle vine, securely wrapped, each stone a separate package in jungle moss. The centuries-old, cold stone castle hovered in the moist, warm foggy vapors, silent, like a ruin at the bottom of the ocean, like a scene from the depths of the Big Sea.

It had twenty-seven rooms and antechambers, three corner turrets and one medium-tall tower. Circling around the once nobel structure ran a moat both deep and wide, filled with the irradiant runoff from the distant caves of the most mysterious Nth Degree. Beside the medium-tall windowless tower was a massive, grated metal gate and drawbridge. Fortunately for Harry, the gate was open and the bridge was down. Indeed, as he approached he could see that the bridge had been down and the gate open for a very long time. In fact, the wooden drawbridge was secured in place by trees hundreds of feet tall that at one time had been but tiny burls attached to the rough underplanking used in the bridges original construction.

As Harry threaded his way between the massive trees of redwood and across the bridge, there was no fear in his heart, for he intuitively felt that peace reigned in this ancient place. He could feel it clinging to the walls like condensation. He walked through the open rusted gate and into a wide central courtyard.

"Hello!" he yelled, listening to his voice roll through the cold stony interior of the apparently empty castle. "Hello!" he yelled again, listening for the echo. "I've been sent to this place by Sir Vain, the White Knight!"

"And who," came a booming reply, "is this Sir Vain creature that he should fling open my noble door to youthful transients of dubious origin?"

Harry observed someone standing in the shadows on the far side of the courtyard. As he looked closer, he could see an old man standing proud, his luxurious, long white hair and beard extending out and around his face like crystals of ice, high in an autumn sky. His rather short, thin body was wrapped in an overlong, dirty black robe and he stood looking at Harry, impatiently tapping one foot. He looked more like a foolish old hobo than the rightful master of this once noble estate. The old man beckoned towards Harry with a long thin hand and turning, disappeared through a heavy wooden door. Harry followed through the door and down a dark entryway into the main part of the castle and emerged in a large room brightly lit with candles, torches and oil lamps. In the center of the room was a long dining table, surrounded by at least fifty high-backed wooden chairs. Heavy tapestries depicting heroic scenes from ancient times adorned all the walls. Directly opposite the entryway, against the far wall, four, high stone steps led up to a platform and upon the platform sat a large intricately carved wooden throne. The old graybeard stood beside the throne.

"Well?" he inquired. "Who are you and what of this Sir Vain creature you speak of?" The old man stood impatiently with his hands on his hips waiting for the booming echo of his own voice to subside.

As Harry launched into his explanation the gray beard began to pace and strut upon the stage, growing ever more impatient. In his practiced poses and rehearsed expressions of peevish impatience, Harry thought he detected an accomplished actor unashamed. Though his body was indeed frail, his form seemed to contain a strong and vital energy that sustained him in smooth, cat-like movements that separated and defined his carefully practiced series of foolish old man stances and poses. Like an ancient Peter Pan or a cynical Santa Claus, he was a most resourceful wizard constantly grinning off sparks from the corners of his eyes. It was his eyes that gave him away, for there was an irony in the lines circling there about, folding back upon themselves in the memory of once recorded laughter.

Finally the old wizard interrupted Harry with a feigned expression of total exasperation. "I have no idea what you are talking about, young man, but I can assure you that there is no White Knight!"

"But I can assure you, sir, I met him! He told me his name was Sir Vane the Avenger, and that he lived in this castle!"

"My dear boy, this individual you encountered in the forest, was he dressed in a white smock and riding an old white plow horse?"

"Plow horse! Sir, the horse he was riding was a most fearsome beast, certainly not a plow horse and as far as his clothing, I can assure you that he was wearing white heavy metal scales and not a smock!"

"My dear boy, how you exaggerate. What an imagination. The person you encountered in the forest was undoubtedly my personal man servant."

"But, he told me his name was Sir Vane, the Avenger."

"Now you do exaggerate. He probably just said he was 'serving the avenger.' I am the avenger and he is my servant. Quite simple now, don't you see? He was just playing."

"But sir, when he rescued me from the Black Knight, he certainly wasn't playing!"

"Of course he was," said the old wizard in a loud booming voice. "Or rather, he was attempting to play. You see, my servant has a fine and noble heart, but his mental growth has been neglected, which is not to say he is crazed, no, no, that's quite another matter; rather, he is stuck at the level of '*Ambition*'".

"Ambition?" Harry inquired.

"Yes," said the old one, "*Survival, Ambition, Love* and *Play*, now don't you know--the *Four Steps to Ecstasy*. The five movements which compose the human symphony or the five acts that make up the human comedy."

"No," Harry said, feeling estranged from what was apparently common knowledge. "I'm afraid I've never heard of the *'Four Steps.'*"

The old man looked at him in utter disbelief. "Yes, yes, you understand. Of course you do! I understand what I am saying perfectly well and if I understand, you certainly understand! Do you understand what I am saying?"

Harry seated himself on one of the high-backed chairs that lined the long table. The old man sauntered down from the dais and began to pace back and forth in front of Harry explaining what he already understood, but didn't realize he understood. Harry felt the need to interrupt the man and establish one important point.

"Excuse me, sir, but I really am completely lost."

The wizard stopped in mid-stride and turned towards him with laughing eyes and an expression of mock horror.

"Lost, you say? My, my, that is a problem."

"Yes, it is. I mean, I'm sorry to interrupt but really...I'm afraid I've lost my way. I have no idea where I am, nor am I even sure how I managed to find myself so lost."

"Is that so?"

Harry nodded seriously and then started to smile, realizing that the old man was putting him on. At the first sign of his smile, his host abruptly stepped back and struck a dramatic pose with one hand clasped compassionately across his chest. He then began to speak as if he were a politician delivering a speech .

"My good man, life is a veritable bog of petty annoyances and minor distractions, all intent on capturing our attention and thereby diverting the errant spirit from its rightful path..."

"Yes sir! That is certainly how it seems to me."

The old wizard looked quizzically at Harry. "Is that so?" he said, slowly stroking his long white beard. "And where was it that you were before you became ah...lost?"

"Oh..." Harry said, "I'm afraid I've been lost for a long while. But I seem to remember...an old house high on a hill."

"You don't say?" rejoined the old graybeard raising his voice dubiously. "A likely story. Why, I bet there really isn't even any such place."

"Oh, yes there is. Of that I'm sure."

"Now, now I'm sure you think there is such a place, but I suspect that it is more apt to be found within your head than upon any specific piece of ground. And if 'home,' as you remember it, is in your head, then I ask you, how could you ever be lost? Just remember young man, wherever you go, there you are."

"But then there is really no such thing or place as home?"

"On the contrary," replied his host with a sly smile. "Everywhere you go, wherever you find yourself, anywhere you can even imagine...is home."

"Why, that is comforting," said Harry, "but hard to believe."

"The truest things in life are often the hardest to believe," said the wizard with a wink. "It is easy to imagine the dreadful, the horrid, the threatening. But just to cast your eyes upon the world and see a veil of gloom doesn't make it true, just easy." And with another wink, he swirled his dirty black robe around him like an ermine cape and immediately stumbled over a nearby chair. "It all depends upon how you look at it."

Suddenly he leaped up and straddled a nearby bench as if it were an unruly horse. "You see," he continued, "one person might become lost in the mere act of survival, while to another, survival would pose no challenge, rather his own ambition might prove to be his undoing. So it goes with love, play and even ecstasy!"

Harry smiled. "Yes, of course, the four steps to Ecstasy."

The old man smiled back, "Now you've got it! Now you've got it."

"Oh, but I'm not sure I do." Harry said.

"But of course you do," said the wizard, resuming his pacing. "At least you remembered, it's almost the same thing. It's just that you don't see what you truly understand. We see what we once understood and we see what we wish to know. Very few of us ever really see what we understand at the moment." He paused to stroke his beard. "We never see the step we are presently standing on, only the one in front and the one to the rear."

"Ahhh..." Harry said with gradual realization. "As I climb the stairs I fill which ever step I stand on, thus I only see the one in front and the one immediately behind?"

"Exactly! What did I tell you, eh?" The little old man took a small bow and then dashed across the spacious hall with the agility of a quick grey fox. He ran alongside the large table, across the tiled floor and up the four steps to his throne.

Harry stood and approached the throne, "But sir..." he said in a rather loud, but respectful voice. "I still say Sir Vane was not playing out there in the forest when he rescued me from the Black Knight!"

The wizard spun around and fell smoothly backwards into its time honored softness of his throne.

"Of course, you do. I'm not deaf! It's quite obvious to me what you say, and why you say it! Now approach the throne."

Harry moved tentatively forward, feeling as if he was within the grip of some powerful force field.

"No, no!" said the graybeard. "Come even closer and I will show you what you know, but cannot see. Stand upon the first step."

"Now, you are standing on the first step and it is called Survival...eh?"

Harry nodded
.

"So, look in front of you and behind you and tell me what you see."

Harry looked to the front and to the rear and then recited his observations in a high, clear voice, like the attentive student that he imagined himself to be. "In front of me I see the next step is Ambition and behind me I see...oblivion."

"Exactly right! Now, take the next step and tell me what you see."

Obediently, Harry stepped up and felt himself relax. "Why, I see Survival behind me and Love next in store."

The old man feigned limp applause, "Very good. Very good! And now..." He motioned and the young man ascended yet another step.

"Now I see Ambition as a thing of the past and Play ahead of me as my desire."

The wizard smiled.

"Oh," Harry said. "I see what you say now! This third step is where your man servant stands."

"Exactly correct!" said the old man, standing and abruptly whipping off his dirty robe with a flourish and carefully laying it over the arm of his throne. Beneath his robe he wore a magnificently beaded shirt with curious patterns. "His only reality is his past, thus he sees himself as stuck in the rather sticky realm of Ambition!"

"Ah ha," Harry said as if suddenly discovering the source of a rather annoying noise. "But his real desire is to play. So you help him to play..."

The old man reseated himself once again upon his throne. "You need not specify 'real,' young man. There is no degree to desire. Desire either is or it isn't! But yes, you are essentially correct. You see, since he relies on a past level of awareness to point the direction toward a future desired goal, he wishes me to assign him tasks so that he might win over the challenge of the task and thus realize his ambition."

"That must wear you out, thinking up things for him to do."

"Yes indeed, yes indeed! You're catching on, and you're right, of course. A dismal prospect thinking up continual tasks. So, one fine day I decided to cut directly to the root of the matter and assign him a perpetual task. I say perpetual task, which is what play is in essence...a perpetual task!"

"You mean tracking down the elusive Black Knight?"

"Balderdash!" said the wizard explosively. "I most assuredly do not mean tracking down any such thing! I don't wish to startle you, I mean, don't become faint, but you still don't seem to catch on...there is no Black Knight!"

"But..." Harry said. "The black arrow? I saw it!"

"The arrow, the arrow...a rose by any other name would still stink of sweet romance and bitter intrigue. It's all in the name, my good man." He crooked his index finger toward Harry and bent over. "A secret, my friend, as well as a riddle: If there were such a thing as creativity and if such a creature were to have a home, where do you think it would live? On the fourth step, of course! Play and creation are synonymous expressions describing the same activity. So..." he continued in hushed tones. "One fine morning, when my servant came to me in hope of cajoling me into assigning him yet another meaningless task, I happened to unobtrusively place the black arrow in his pack. It was the same one that you observed in the forest. He discovered it, of course, and came directly to me with the wicked-looking wand and asked my impression. Well, I examined it closely and looked at it most studiously and then handed it back to him and said...'Hummm, what do you make of it?' From that day forth, he has never bothered to ask me for another assigned task."

Harry had to smile. "You mean he invented the Black Knight?"

The old man nodded with a smile. "Everything! The armor, weapons, horse vestments...the full catastrophe!"

"But that is certainly remarkable!"

"Not so remarkable, look where he was standing."

And Harry looked down at the step he occupied: it was, of course, the third step...Love.

"Though his desire is to play," said the wizard, "and though his past lies with Ambition, it is the space of Love that his innate awareness presently occupies and love, at least in the initial stages, can be a vengeful and creative master. Thus, with nothing more substantial than a single black arrow, he became the White Knight: Sir Vain, my avenger and protector!"

"And all of that came from just the one black arrow-amazing."

"Not so amazing when you think that universes have started with less..."

"But surely, he must realize by now that there is no Black Knight?"

"One would assume," said the wizard, carefully placing his hands upon the arms of his throne, "since it was he who shot the black bolt at you!"

"And he could have killed me! How was I to know there wasn't any Black Knight?"

"How indeed!" chuckled the old man, "Wouldn't be any fun if you both knew. Let me tell you, though, I don't think it is play for him. No, I can assure you of that. I'm afraid he will have little realization of play for a long while yet. We are still witnessing the Ambition he utilizes to fuel his Love, in order to ah...play."

Harry looked into the wizard's wrinkled face. It had as many lines as a cross-sectioned log from an unbearably ancient tree. He took another step up towards the platform.

"Who are you, anyway? Or maybe I should ask, 'what' are you?"

He slowly cleaned his pipe and looked up from time to time at Harry standing brightly on the fourth step. He admitted only to having once been a specialist in 'pre-war reality;' an organizer of divergent opinions and other people's prejudices. Made a fortune once changing lead into gold. Harry pressed him for details, but he immediately cut the traveler short.

"Let's just say that what I once was, I was. The important thing to remember is that I am...now! In fact, I am what I am as much as possible."

When pressed for his proper name, he once again evaded the subject.
"And what is it to you, my young friend? Making a list? Writing a book?"

"Why no, but it is just proper to exchange names when meeting a new person. I find it helps immeasurably in remembering one's past experiences to be able to connect a specific event with a particular name."

"Young man," replied the old man with a rueful glance, "there are only three reasons why any reasonable person would ever have need of a proper name. One, if he were accustomed to using the public mails. And two, if he habitually frequented crowded places. I do neither."

"And?"

"And what?"

"You said there were three reasons. What's the third?"

The old graybeard looked Harry directly in the eye, "I forget!" he said.

"You forget? How could anyone forget something as important as the third most important reason for having a proper name?"

He stood up and dramatically pointed his pipe at Harry like a small gun.

"Look. I'll remember you as a fourth level vagabond on an ecstasy quest and you can remember me as a playful, foolish old goat, sitting on the throne of ecstasy dreaming of a timeless place! Is it a deal?"

Harry glanced down at the level on which he was standing and then up at the old man seated in his high chair and realized that a truth had been shared.

The wizard observed his moment of inner reflection. "Listen, Harry, let me give you some advice. In case you haven't noticed yet, the transition stages are the hardest. When you are going up or coming down, you are vulnerable--the window is open. When the elevator is moving, there are no doors between floors. The blast of reality will blow right through! Sometimes it will blow right through you and other times it will blow you right through, to the other side of the maze where all things are...different."

Suddenly the old man smiled and begin to fumble around in his pockets like a mime in an old time movie. For the first time, Harry consciously noted the small, clear glass pipe that the old man had been holding in his hand.

"Say, ah," said the wizard, nervously patting his empty pockets. "I seem to have misplaced my smoke..." He looked woefully at Harry and rolled his eyes in imitation of a bowery bum. "You wouldn't happen to have any, ah...extra?"

Harry stepped forward, only too glad to assist, but as he started to lift his left foot onto the platform that held the throne, the old man stopped him with a shriek!

"Look out! Easy now. My good fellow, if you step one, I say, one foot upon this stone platform, you'll quickly turn into a frog or worse," his hand fluttered through the air, "a bat! And," said the wizard with an upward glance, "goodness knows there are certainly enough of those furry little creatures around here already!"

As Harry glanced up into the smoky gloom that hovered about the wide wooden beams of the roof, he could detect what appeared to be the animated flicker of hundreds, perhaps thousands of the small sullen black forms.

At that very instant the old man quickly scampered down off his throne, almost knocking Harry over, and assumed a seat at the long table in the center of the room. When Harry regained his balance, he withdrew the pouch and handed the last remaining leaf to the wizard. The old man looked rather doubtfully at the mixture and then tentatively sniffed it as if it were the decaying remains of an exotic animal. He shook his head, wrinkled his nose and quickly tossed a sizable pinch over his left shoulder and then touched a second pinch to the tip of his tongue.

Harry watched in surprise. He was about to voice his objections to the old man for wasting his last remaining leaf when suddenly the wizard smiled, as if satisfied, and began to cheerfully pack his pipe.

"Never can be too careful these days!" he uttered with searing conviction.

Harry nodded. As the wizard touched flame to pipe, he leaned back comfortably in his chair and lifted his feet up onto the table, motioning for Harry to do the same.

From the courtyard, they suddenly heard the agonized roar of a lion.

"It's the lizard," the kindly old gentleman said with a wink, "thinks he's a dog."

After a few moments of silence, he blew a satisfying stream of smoky vapor between his yellowed teeth, handed Harry the pipe and said, "You may call me...*And*."

Harry looked at him. "And what?"

"And, nothing. Just *AND*! You wanted a name, a cage, a container, a mental recovery symbol for your idea and memory of me, so think of and refer to me as...*AND*."

"But I don't think I understand." Harry said. "What sort of a name is *AND*? It doesn't even mean anything? It doesn't make any sense."

The wizard peered at him through the smoky blue haze.

"At least I don't think it means anything..." Harry said, wavering beneath the wizard's steady gaze. "I could be wrong..."

The wizard continued to stare at him through an apparently never ending stream of smoky possibility and rising expectation.

"So, O.K.!" Harry said, abandoning prior prejudice and making the blind intellectual leap necessary to transform a conjunction into a proper noun. "'*And*' it is!" And suddenly, somehow, it seemed to fit. "By the way, my name is *Harry*," he added quickly, almost as an after thought. "Glad to meet you."

"By the lizard, there's only one creature that's got leaf like this!" *And* suddenly rocked forward in his chair, dropping his feet to the floor and bringing his fist down hard upon the wooden table with a resounding smack! "By Jove, this smoke is smooth! This calls for a drink. What do you say? Got time for a drink?"

Harry nodded affirmatively and fearing that And hadn't heard him, he announced yet again, "By the way my name is Harry and..."

And's hand slapped down explosively upon the table once again as he erupted in laughter. "I know who you are, boy. I also know where you are from and, I might add, I even know where you are going." At that point his laughter erupted in short ominous bursts, like fire from an automatic weapon, threatening to send him tumbling from his chair.

And then stood up and began shouting. "Where is he?" he bellowed, slapping the large refectory table like a gong.

"Where is who?" Harry inquired.

"Where is *Who*?" said And. "Who, indeed!"

And with that, the old wizard collapsed into his chair which immediately tipped over backward, sending its occupant sprawling.

Harry leapt to his feet just as the old man's head popped into view over the table's edge.

"Sir Vain is *Who!* My White Knight, my champion, my...wine steward! That's who! Ah, ha, ha, ha..." And down again he went in a fit of uncontrollable laughter.

Harry had to laugh. "Where are you going?" he said, observing And crawling across the cold stone floor on his hands and knees.

"Where is *Who* going?" replied And, innocently.

Harry was now laughing hard.

"No," he said, "*Who* is out playing."

At that, And began to laugh so hard, he fell over on his back and began to kick and paw at the air. "Ahhhhh, ha,ha...no, no. He that is 'Who' is out searching. It is you and I that are playing!"

"But who are you...really?" Harry said, suddenly serious again.

"Ah, ha, ha," laughed And, struggling to his feet. "That is really funny. Who am I, indeed. Certainly not an open ended question- ah, ha, ha, ha!"

And with that he ran from the room, holding his side with one hand while trying to slip on his dirty black robe with the other. As he departed the room, Harry picked up the fallen chair and slid it back into place. And's head suddenly popped back into view around the corner of the doorway. "Be back in a *FLASH*!" he said and as Harry stared in utter disbelief, there was a brilliant flash of light and And miraculously stood before him holding a cut crystal decanter of amber fluid in his gnarled old hands. "You look like a man who could use a drink," he said, matter-of-factly.

"How did you do that?" Harry asked.

"How did who do what?" replied the wizard with a sly smile.

The young man was astonished. "How did you do that? With the flash of light?"

And looked at him and began to laugh again.

"No," Harry said, "Seriously, I mean how were you able to vanish and then reappear in front of me holding that decanter?"

And looked sternly at him and shook his finger in mock

admonishment. "Tsk, tsk, tsk, my liege. Haven't you yet realized that there are no truths, no dragons, no...serious?"

And shook his head sadly and walked to the table and set the decanter down beside two clear-cut, crystal goblets which had quite mysteriously appeared. "If it truly be '*serious*,' that you desire, Harry, I can assure you that there is world enough, as well as time, and if you should find that even that be not enough, then rest assured you've but to die, and eternity will gladly offer up the necessary space for you to fill with your...'*seriousness*!' I kindly request, though, that as long as you are within these hallowed halls, please refrain from uttering that word! Do I make myself clear?"

Harry was stunned, as well as a little ashamed, for once again he knew in his heart that his vanity had managed to slip between that which he truly desired and that which he had merely observed. He also felt that somewhere behind the raucous laughter of And was a level of reality whose gravity made his own '*seriousness*' appear quite absurd.

While Harry was thus lost in reflection, And had began to slowly fill the two goblets with the dark amber fluid. As Harry watched, he felt the tension in the air, and in a sincere attempt to break the mood, he uttered a rather brash reply to And's request.

"And what if I don't," he muttered satirically, "refrain from being serious?"

And looked up at him in disbelief, as if he had been slapped. Then the deep furrows etched in his face began to deepen and bend slowly into a simple, peaceful smile-indeed, a living model of the very first smile.

"If you don't," said And quite simply, "I'll merely transform you instantaneously into a *real human being* and compel you to take tap dancing lessons along with the rest of the company!" And with that he winked and handed Harry a glass full of the dark fluid.

"To the *Dreamer of All That Is*," he said raising his glass in toast. "May his sleep be pleasant and untroubled."

Harry raised his glass also. "*To the Dreamer of All That Is!*"

And of course after the first toast, came a second, and then a third, and then...

***

CHAPTER TEN

"And"
Part Two

A large tawny long haired cat with green flashing eyes sauntered into the main hall and over And's drunken prostrate form with scarcely a flicker of recognition. The bushy blonde feline then stalked directly over to Harry, rubbed up once against his leg, gave him a high arching glance, and with a low moan was gone; out of the room, down the hall and up the steep, sudden stairs immediately beyond the big double doors. Harry was up on his feet and moving out the door and up the stairs after the cat, all thoughts of the old wizard and the past evening's drinking bout having suddenly evaporated from his mind like bubbles from the top of a glass of cheap champagne.

By the time he topped the stairs, he observed the cat, half way down a long hall, glance back over its shoulder with a withering look and then dart through a small, grey, oaken door at the very end of the gloom-darkened passage. Harry quickly followed and, ducking low through the door, found himself to be in a small, circular, cold stone room. Suddenly the door through which he had just passed slammed shut with a harsh brittle snap, plunging him into total darkness. It was as if someone had snatched his eyes from out of his head. The darkness so surprised him that he inadvertently moaned, and in that moaning, he distinctly heard a second moan. And then there was a flash of light so bright it fell like an explosion in a drunkard's tomb, illuminating a narrow staircase that climbed up towards the ceiling, where there was another door. It was small and metal and slowly opening. The door continued to open until the spreading beam of light fell full upon his face and then it stopped and began to draw him up the stairs slowly, one step at a time, like a warm fog rising off a cool sea. Finally, as if hypnotized, Harry reached the top stair and extended his hand toward the partially open door when a husky female voice cried out.

"Don't touch that door, traveler!"

His hand jumped back as if it had received a strong electrical shock
.
"Who are you and what is it that you could possibly want from me?" The smooth syrupy voice then erupted into laughter rich in erotic implication and promise. "As if I didn't know..."

Harry stood dumbstruck in front of the black metal door and recited his name and mission like a tradesman lost in a strange town on a very dark and remote street. As he finished, he found that he was shivering from the cold draft that seemed to emanate from beyond the partially opened door. He stepped forward once again and extended his hand only to be stopped again by the voice.

"Stay your hand, gypsy, and do not enter this space, for the cold you feel now is nothing compared to the cold you will feel if you enter this room."

"But who are you?" Harry inquired, feeling as if he were drugged or perhaps asleep.

She laughed, "Don't get impatient, Harry. Our time will come, but our time is not yet and it must not be forced. It is I who will come to you, my young friend, and not the other way around. It is Desire's only daughter who lays in wait in the white heat of passion for her prey. My quest is for gratification--immediate and personal. I eat humans and swallow the seed, but right now I have no appetite for dreamers. Your yearning is for the stuff that forms universes and art. You don't seek union with a woman. Your desire will not be satiated short of a mystic union with the Dreamer of All That Is. Now leave here and forget about this room. It is a dank, cold space that should not be frequented by young visionaries."

And with that, the door eased shut with a metallic snap that caused him to shudder. Once again he stood in darkness, his sight momentarily plucked from his consciousness, leaving him blind with nothing but the memory of a low, husky female voice, rich and throaty in its vibrant implication and soft promise.

Meanwhile, downstairs, it was a new day. And was up and about, moving through the cold, stony lonesomeness of his castle just as he moved through the warm brilliance of his own consciousness and that was, in a word, effortlessly. With but one body to share, And was a close knit family, parent, adult, and child. The movement between these three facets of self was a fluid and joyful celebration. The silken fibers of And's imaginings were spun by a delicate hand. To be in the presence of the man spewing out his statements or laboring at his tasks was to witness a living realization of rhythm and harmony. To be with And was to be in the presence of a creator, for the way he danced out his life was art, which is not to say that his life was particularly beautiful. In fact, when Harry later entered the main hall and stood quietly watching And feed large logs into the gigantic stone fireplace, he marveled at how such an extraordinary character could be housed in such a dismal, damp and cluttered house. For in truth, the roof leaked, moss grew on some of the interior walls, and, stacked helter skelter throughout the width and breadth of the structure, were boxes and piles and piles and boxes of what could only be described as...*stuff*! Extra thoughts no doubt, as yet unneeded, but lying in wait and occupying physical form, ready for some "*might be, could be*" tomorrow. Stacks and piles of answers to as yet unasked questions.

"Where have you been?" asked And turning from the massive fireplace and rubbing his hands together in appreciation of the sudden warmth.

"I've just come from the tower," Harry said, entering the room and seating himself on the plush red velvet couch that stood in front of the fireplace.

"You don't say..." said And slowly twirling his long white moustache. "And what, may I ask, did you find in the tower?"

"The woman. Desire's only daughter," Harry said, watching the flames leaping about.

"What woman?" inquired And with wide eyes.

Harry looked up from the fire. "What woman?"

"Yes," said And. "What woman? What did she look like?"

"Well," Harry said, "I didn't really see her, you see..."

"So!" said And casually interrupting him and turning back toward the fire, "you didn't meet her."

"But I did!" Harry said. "I spoke with her and she spoke with me."

And turned towards him. "But you didn't meet her," he said with much gravity. "You have known me because I am a foolish old man and you can see a *'me to be,'* but the lady in the tower is a different matter entirely. In your present position, there is no reason for you to meet Desire's only daughter, save beyond a heavy metal door in the uppermost tower room of an ancient stone structure imagined by a youthful visionary on the track of a dream."

Harry leaned back heavily into the massive red couch. "But, I talked with her and she answered with a voice and thoughts of her own. She was very nice and I'm sure I would recognize her if and when we should ever meet again."

"Did you perhaps catch sight of her shadow as it passed by the crack beneath the door?"

"Well, no..."

"Then how would you recognize her?"

"Well, perhaps through her distinctive voice?"

And frowned slightly, "And what would that tell you?"

"It would tell me that she was the daughter of Desire, the very same one I spoke with this day in the tower of And's castle."

"Ah, my young friend," said the old graybeard as he stood down from the fireplace. "The creature you are speaking of is *Lust* and it does not reside in the soft lilt of a young woman's voice nor does it inhabit the tower room of this stony residence. And, for all your perceptual acuity, you will not have the luxury of observing its approach. Should you encounter *Lust* in *'real life,'* rest assured that it will not be through the eyes of a visionary, for Lust is not an observable outer phenomenon, but an intense inner force that comes not as a friend with glad hand extended, nor as a lover with open heart, but as a furtive spy in the night, nostrils flared, eyes raging, intent on grabbing your total attention by its primordial root and shaking you back to your primitive past."

And hesitated for a moment to make sure that Harry was paying proper attention. "Once you make the sudden acquaintance of *Lust*, my young friend, you will never again mistake her for another, for she is a most impolite visitor. When *Lust* comes to call, she never knocks."

Harry shook his head in disbelief. "Come on now, surely you exaggerate. She certainly didn't sound anything like that to me. In fact, she sounded perfectly fine."

And sat down next to Harry on the couch and spoke to him most sincerely. "The only thing '*fine*' about *Lust*, Harry, is her fickle restlessness. If her sudden appearance should ever cause you to become anxious, take heart in the knowledge that she will not stay long, and try to relax and draw comfort from her leaving and not from her coming..."

Harry folded his arms behind his head and looked up toward the ceiling. He found this all very strange and hard to believe. "If what you say is true, then why would I have even thought that I met and conversed with this creature?"

And shrugged. "Your desire led you here to this old stony fortress so that you might be allowed a rest, a point of reference, a brief, if illusory respite on your trek between the quick and the dead. Likewise your imagination placed the idea of a female held captive high in a tower. Why you chose Lust only you can answer. Perhaps it is still simmering somewhere on a back burner or maybe it will present itself eventually in a form other than female. Remember, Harry, that Lust is an evolutionary part of a human's nature and can assume any shape. Why, in some places in space, it is rumored that people have even lusted after inanimate objects..."

"Objects?" Harry found this incomprehensible.

"Sure," said And. "Automobiles, stereophonic sound systems, real estate, stocks and bonds, jewelry, Money! Why, in certain advanced societies--towards the end--people even lusted after initials like *M.D., Phd, DDS, LLD, MA, BA,* and even *AA*."

Harry smiled and nodded his head as if to acknowledge that the pathways encountered in the mind of man were simply beyond comprehension. "Anything is possible..." he said, "Anything is possible. But what about you, my friend? *The Geni of Desire* made no mention of you either."

And smiled, "And that is to your credit and as it should be, for both Desire and And are but aspects of the vision, Harry, and not the other way around. You do not merely sit passively like a clerk checking off a list of events called your life! The soul's sense of vision is the crystal, Harry. *The Geni of Desire*, as well as myself, are but two of the many necessary facets that must be cut in order for the crystal to refract the light of *The Dreamer*. The glare and flicker of brilliance from the stone, is simply your life, lived! This whole castle experience is a seed, an idea placed within your mind by the Geni and brought into being when watered by your own willful intent. Desire saw it as a sort of bench, for you to rest upon within the dense inner ring of your park-like imagination after having traversed the very distracting forest of Content."

Harry sat open mouthed, listening to the voice of And echoing down through the corridors of his young mind.

"You are a questor," said And quietly. "The seeds have been planted. You have it within you to become a jeweler in consciousness. But, listen to me run on." He stood and motioned for Harry to stand also. "Now, you've had your rest and it's time for you to continue with your journey." He touched him on the top of his head and then turned and made a motion towards the fire. "Never forget to speak the truth; remember that truth is a fire, and to speak truthfully means to shine and to burn!"

The fireplace popped and crackled and snapped and Harry was shocked into apparent wakefulness, as if from a very deep reverie, and so it was that he found himself walking rather casually alongside the purple infrared stream still playing his red bamboo flute. As he glanced about, he was surprised to see that he must have been walking in a trance for quite a long while, for the distant, white rock cliff was no longer on the far horizon. In fact, it was now no more than a mile away and he could clearly see the large open cave that loomed at the base of the stone edifice like a gaping open mouth.

***

CHAPTER ELEVEN

"The caves of Nth Degree and the Lake of Illusion"

On the opposite side of the stream, Harry spied a quick movement through the dense greenery and was surprised to see a young boy emerge from the vines all wet and dripping as if he had just crawled from the chill dampness of the purple fluid. Soon the child passed. And then, after awhile, Harry noticed another child and then a pair. They seemed to be quite happy, some alone, some arm in arm, boys and girls together playing their way downstream, passing quite close to him and yet apparently unaware of his presence and completely oblivious to his passing. There seemed to be some sort of invisible barrier that prevented their seeing him, for, time and time again, one or another of the children would pass close enough for him to reach out and touch. At these times they would look in his direction and yet not sense his presence. Gradually, as he drew nearer to the entrance to the cave, he noticed that the children became younger and younger. By the time he stood just outside the mouth of the large cavern, the children had become mere babies gurgling and cooing sounds of bliss and contentment, seemingly bubbling up from the large pool that filled the yawning mouth of the cave. Overhead, the sheer face of the cliff rose high into the air, beyond his field of perception.

Curious and still somewhat dumbfounded by his recent encounter with And, Harry felt himself subtly drawn around the pool with its gurgling babies and into the very mouth of the cave. As he entered, the first thing he noticed was the cold. After the warm, humid vapors of the jungle, the inside of the cavern was freezing. Moving toward the rear of the cave, he noticed a small passage at the very back lit by a pale glow of unknown origin. He hesitated at the start of the passage and wondered what new manner of strangeness was sure to lay ahead.

He stood silently appraising his odds of ever reaching his desired goal when he felt a gentle nudge against his right leg. He glanced down and saw that one of the babies from the pool had strayed the pack. As he stooped to recover the child, a shrill voice commanded him in harsh tones, "Don't you dare contaminate that child with your earthly stench!"

Harry jumped in surprise and quickly looked about for the source of the sound. At first, he could see nothing in the shadowy darkness, but then the sound of high pitched breathing drew his eye to the very rear of the passage and there, lit by the vague glow from some distant beyond, stood the creature. It was a very small, rubbery-looking ugly doll, all pasty damp and pale as death with long, scraggly hair hanging in damp ringlets about its little hunched shoulders. It stood with its fists clenched at its sides, heaving its chest and emitting wheezing sounds as if it were terribly afraid or terribly mad. The only color displayed upon the otherwise pale body were two aqua-blue lines drawn horizontally beneath the creatures deep-set black eyes, giving it the look of some outraged, aboriginal pygmy warrior. Harry leaned over to peer at the creature in the passage way. The little man (without benefit of cloth concealment, there was no doubt regarding its sex) stood no higher than twelve inches, possibly fourteen on its tiptoes.

"I beg your pardon?" Harry answered, squinting into the darkness. The little man stood shaking in frustrated rage and then delivered an explosive two minute monologue which ended when he abruptly turned and stalked off down the dimly lit passageway. Harry was most confused. The creature's language and his own were obviously the same because he clearly understood the last phrase uttered to be "*FOLLOW ME*!" delivered in the voice of an adult male, but the lengthy part preceding the first phrase was totally indecipherable. At times, the creature's voice sounded like the mating plea of a humpbacked whale, while at other times, it sounded like a phonograph record slowing to a gradual stop. At some points, it would begin a phrase sounding like a young woman, only to end the same phrase sounding exactly like a very old man. Most confusing and difficult to follow.

What Harry did not realize, of course, was that he had

inadvertently stumbled into the ice caverns presided over by that infamous character known as *Nth Degree*, the sometimes transparent, sometimes opaque thought-form who, chameleon-like, was able to take on the emotional color and hue of that which surrounded him. He was an amorphous, plastic-fantastic entity that grows and glows and shrinks and gives off curious odors that ranged from subtly pleasant to most foul indeed. His size seemed to be determined by the company he kept. Around individuals of relative innocence, he might appear to be quite small, whereas when in the company of the perverted or the obsessed, he might grow to truly gargantuan proportions. It was as if his nature fed off the negative energy of others. To some, the caverns of colored ice presided over by Nth Degree might be compared to Hades, with Nth Degree as the devil incarnate or the grim reaper-Death! But, nothing would be further from the truth, for in the ice caverns there was no death, there were merely those poor individuals who had become trapped for a time in the vise-like grip of their own worst passions and prejudices-prisoners of their own device. These were the deluded ones who had stopped somewhere along the road of life and for whom life had suddenly become a prison instead of a prism. These individuals thus became the walking dead marching in slow time. Each and every one a prison of trapped light and color, shadow and substance, a veritable Pompeii in colored ice. These were men and women caught mid-stride somewhere along the road of life and abruptly projected here and apparently frozen within the specific color of their particular passion. Together, they constituted the army of the ages passing through eternity, for in the caves of *Nth Degree* there was no speech spoken, no music heard, no laughter, no song of celebration, no minor victories and no death...only dying.

Into this cheerless salon of frozen suffering Harry walked, following the trail of Nth Degree. Finally, after the initial shock, for Nth Degree wasn't used to observing individuals walk into his domain, he graciously agreed to lead Harry on a tour of the cavern maze, with the private hope, no doubt, of placing him in an appropriate alcove somewhere within the multi-leveled catacombs. In the course of the tour Harry learned that each level of the subterranean complex harbored entities of bolder and more vibrant color and combinations of color. Whereas the upper levels seemed to house individuals of relatively pale coloration, the lower levels held the brighter and more vibrant colors until some poor souls stood frozen in mid-stride like multicolored birds-- veritable peacocks in colored ice, with each and every color signaling an intense and very specific flaw and obsession. But though these people were frozen, they were not hopelessly stuck: there was a way out. Over time, perhaps hundreds of years, each entity would have the opportunity to examine his or her own problems, and gradually, through understanding, become one unified color or another and then, by diminishing the intensity of their individual color, process up through the levels until they finally became as clear and innocent once again as children and went spilling out of the cave mouth in the infrared stream of emotional run-off. At that point, as children, they would flow out and over the countryside to irrigate humankind with a truer sense of what is, as well as what can be, for though loneliness will make you strong, in the end, it is only love that will set you free.

As they descended through the lower levels, Nth Degree began to expand in size, as if gaining sustenance from the frozen ones standing about, here and there, in the small alcoves and passageways. In time, he became monstrous in size, like a gas-filled balloon filling all the available space. Harry soon found himself pressed against the wall by his host's fleshy body and only by scrunching down along the floor could he catch a brief glimpse of one of the painted bird-like humanoids in the near distance. As they moved through the deeper passages, Nth Degree's speech became lower and slower.

"The light is so bright and we are like prisms," whispered Nth Degree in his husky baritone.

Harry stopped to stare open-mouthed as Nth Degree pointed out specific examples of these human crystals, glittering with brilliant light somewhere deep within the earth.

"Aren't the colors stunning!" muttered his host.

Harry could only stare. And each and every one a different color, hue and shade, like hothouse flowers frozen in icy amber.

"Each color has its positive, as well as negative aspects, but in trapped entities, the light does not seem to pass through, but remains trapped within, with seemingly no means of escape. In the egocentric prism, the helpless victim is walled in by the very light which he refracts. The ego dies in its own glass cage, but--" said Nth Degree, gesturing with a long arm suddenly grown grotesquely heavy and dank, "The solution is simple--*LOVE IT*! Embrace it! Surrender to it!" And then, turning to Harry, he delivered his next line in a breathy whisper that smelled like freshly escaped sewer gas from the bowels of Hell. "The reason for the block is also the reason for the breakthrough. Maya is a hard mistress..." he nodded, "stern but just, teaching a difficult lesson; while some things work, others don't, but in the end, when the dreamer finally awakes, it is all just illusion..."

And then at an even lower level, Harry found himself pressed against the floor by the great rolling belly of Nth Degree. As he watched and listened in disbelief, the creature turned its now massive head in his direction, spilling great masses of dank, dark hair like fields of rotting hay, and gesturing down, indicated yet other, even deeper levels where the really "serious" cases were kept.

"Woe the feeble physical envelope that must endure the pressure of that awesome spiritual cramp called mortality!" he said.

Harry felt faint inhaling the vile fumes of Nth Degree's breath and body odor. He longed to be a simple idea and fade away or perhaps a defective electric light and just flicker out. Questions and answers; answers and questions...

Later, at a higher level, where Nth Degree once again resumed more normal physical proportions, Harry explained his quest and how he happened to stumble into the ice caverns. Hearing this, Nth Degree actually began to cry real tears, causing his blue eye makeup (which he wore, he said, to feign indifference) to run down his now reasonably proportioned cheeks.

"Yes!" he said. He too, long, long ago had been on such a quest and "Yes!" he, too, had almost taken his own life on the very same banks of the river Elin and "Yes!" he too had had a similar encounter with the great leather-winged beast that feeds on stray thoughts and becomes reborn within the eternal pool of fire. They were both ecstatic with their great sharing.

"Yes!" cried Nth Degree, he, too, had even constructed an instrument for the creation of music. It was a stringed instrument, and, once in a great while, he would still find an isolated spot within his icy domain where a particularly grief-stricken spirit stood trapped within the confines of its own device and play his music. He had found playing to be the same as praying and he often prayed for those trapped within cells of their own creation.

When Harry inquired why he had remained within the lonely

caverns, Nth Degree explained that when he initially came upon the scene, there was no caretaker and often as not, the babies would drown in their own emotional run-off. Tears fell from his eyes as he recalled witnessing, for the first time, a spiritual entity, long-entrapped within the passion of its own prejudice, finally succeed in thawing itself through the sheer power of love, only to drown as an innocent child in the purple infrared pool. "Well, it was just too much!" he said, "Sort of like watching a caterpillar change into a beautiful butterfly, only to get run over by a truck." And thus he became trapped, as he put it, by his own compassion: tethered to the frozen catacombs by the traces of habit, as surely as any "natural" resident. A psychic lifeguard stationed for eternity alongside a bottomless pool. Quartermaster to The Corps. Supply sergeant to the Army of The Ages. A spiritual midwife assisting in the process of birth and rebirth. A cryogenic technician.

"But why do the babies drown like that? It doesn't seem fair, after all they've been through?"

Nth Degree simply looked at Harry and shrugged his now tiny little shoulders. "That's life."

Harry walked toward the front of the cave, to where the pool extended out into the light, and pointed off down the hill. "Where does the stream go?"

Nth Degree walked up beside him, his little eyes cringing against the bright jungle day. "Well", he said hesitantly, "it flows back down through the *Imagination* until it reaches the forest of *Content* and there, it is absorbed by the deluded ones during periods of deep sleep and becomes known to them as their dreams, their day dreams, as well as their night dreams, and often as not their nightmares."

They both stood by the pool, gazing off down stream, thinking their private thoughts and watching a couple of children playing their way along the shore, frolicking in and out of the bushes.

"And that's it?"

"Oh no," replied Nth Degree, "certainly not. That just implies the beginning of a new cycle. Think of it like rain that falls to the earth and gathers in pools, only to be recycled through evaporation into moisture which forms the cloud. In this case, the cloud of dreams formed by the sleeping ones falls eventually into a great pool that is called the *Lake of Illusion*. It is one large point of condensation. It is one vast reservoir into which flow all the dreams of those who still believe in the sanctity of sleep. And in the middle of the *Lake of Illusion*, there are fourteen ghostly islands. These small, nameless islands are continuously enveloped in a strange bluish fog that whiffs up from the smooth glassy surface of the lake. They sit clustered in the mist like ancient gnarled fingers, extending up through the dreamy vapors of pure illusion. They are separated only by very narrow channels. Warnings from olden times, and before, specifically state that all free men and sons of The Dreamer should be especially wary when trying to thread their way through these foggy straits, for in trying to cross the lake or navigate from island to island, one is apt to become transfixed and hypnotized by the dream-dramas generated within the smooth glassy surface and reflected upward through the bluish mists. If one hesitates and glances down upon the drama unfolding within the Lake of Illusion for even a minute, one will almost certainly become caught up in the veritable sea of mediocrity and drown."

Harry sat on a ledge by the cave mouth and Nth Degree perched next to him on a small rock. From their position they could look out over the stream as it wound its way down the hill and out over miles and miles of jungle.

"And these islands have no names?"

"They have no individual names, only numbers, but collectively, they are referred to as the *TV-Channels*."

Harry thought for a moment. "But what is the purpose of such a horrible sounding place and where is this *Lake of Illusion* located?"

Nth Degree picked up a small, soft blue stone and began

reapplying his eye makeup (which earlier tears had washed away.) "It serves as a buffer zone between the *Imagination* and *Paradise*: between the world of three-dimensional illusion and the world of the spirit. It is *The Gate* through which all have to pass at least once. It is right above us."

"Right above us?"

"Yes, that's correct. Now let me show you the way...."

Harry was incredulous. "Show me the way? Now hold on a minute, my friend. Maybe I just don't want to go there."

Nth Degree casually tossed the blue stone away and looked up at Harry with a feigned expression of utter indifference. "Well," he replied, "you certainly can't stay here and there's no turning back at this point."

Logic always terrified Harry. "Seems like I've heard that before, but why would I even want to go to the *Lake of Illusion* and risk drowning in a *'sea of mediocrity'*?"

"Stop whining. You're just suffering growing pains, spiritual teething. You've got to cross the *Lake of Illusion* and thread your way among the *TV-Channels* in order to enter *Paradise*."

"Ah...Paradise."

Nth Degree looked at Harry with feigned disdain. "Yes, *Paradise* and," he added with great dignity, "on the other side of Paradise, lies *The Big Sea*. In any case," he cautioned, "you must be very, very careful and not utter a sound, least the natural residents of Paradise discover a pretender in their midst. Not good."

"Sounds like risky business to me..."

"Oh, don't worry, you'll find a way, after all, you can only do what you can do as well as you can. Always remember that we're all just babies here, don't you see? We're all just pretenders in the void."

And with the matter settled, Nth Degree proceeded to lead the way down a particularly steep, dark passage. After awhile, Harry began to grow uneasy in the confining space and his breathing became agitated. Finally Nth Degree turned in the tunnel and looked at him.

"Settle down, Harry," he said. "This is a soul exercise, all else is just flash and style. Not to worry, deep down you really know what you're doing."

Somehow this seemed to work and he did settle down and proceeded to take it one step at a time. "Not to worry." As they moved up through a series of switchbacks, Harry asked his guide why he didn't come along to Paradise? Nth Degree answered that he was in paradise as long as he could assist lost souls become reborn to the world of positive experience. Harry nodded thoughtfully in agreement and then, after a while, Nth Degree stopped and pointed ahead. "Go with God, my friend..." he said and then quickly slipped back into the darkness from whence he had come.

With Nth Degree gone Harry was forced to shuffle through the cool stony passage on his knees, feeling his way with his hands. The passage began to narrow, until it seemed to lay like a coiled snake pointing upward at a steep thirty degree angle. Soon the ascent grew so steep that he found himself slipping back, time and time again. For every two feet of forward progress he seemed to slip back one. And then the cool surface of the stone substrata began to feel damp, like the skin of a living thing and then he heard the first of the...sounds. Dull sounds like tennis balls being bounced across a wooden floor, but then later, as the incline grew steeper, the sounds changed. They begin to sound like hard glass marbles being dropped on cement-hundreds of them-and then at the very steepest section, it sounded like he was walking over a couple of inches of shattered glass, breaking it underfoot and creating a sound of squeaking, giving an impression of living sound, like rats. It made the small hairs at the base of his neck stand. He chose not to think about the distraction and focused his mind on placing one foot in front of the other. The slow climbing pace assumed prominence in his mind and he almost succeeded in forgetting the squeaking shrieks in the darkness. Soon the air grew warmer and more humid until the walls of the rocky tunnel were dripping with some liquid substance. And then the stony passage began to grow smaller and tighter, until he had to place both of his arms over his head in order to squeeze along. All about him he felt immense pressure until he was no longer sure if he was crawling through the tunnel or whether the tunnel was digesting him. It was difficult to breathe and impossible to turn back. He began to fear that Nth Degree had played some monstrous trick on him. He felt as if he had been unwittingly fed to the mountain.

And then he thought he saw a light. It was a small light, a pinpoint of brightness somewhere above him and then it was gone and soon the vertical chimney was squeezing him upward like a snake in a tube, or like a fetus in a womb pushing toward the world. And then there was a second light and it was much brighter than the first. It illuminated the innards of the tight constricting tube in a flash, like a cosmic X-ray, and he was once again reminded how much the twisting of the small passage resembled the innards of a gigantic serpent all grayish pink and lined around with tiny ridges like pulsing nerves frozen in stone.

It seemed like Harry had been crawling toward the light for a long while, perhaps days and days, perhaps years. There was no time. He had memory of passing through seven distinct levels or stony plateaus within the passage. At each plateau, there was a flattened spot, no doubt worn away by the fevered bodies of countless other questors. And then, after a suitable rest and period of reflection, he would proceed further along the narrow channel that seemed to contain and squeeze him along like a partially digested seedpod enroute to some particularly disquieting end. As he approached the light he could not help but close his eyes for the light was very bright and continued to grow brighter. It made his eyes water and sting. He felt terribly lonely.

Harry finally crawled, stumbling and tumbling, into the neon brightness of the sudden light like a delinquent roomer evicted into the world or like a human baby born in a hospital. He slowly crawled, panting out of the dark, onto a large flat rock like the first prehistoric swamp creature to make its home on dry land. The light was so intensely bright that for a very long while, he could not open his eyes. And yet even through the skin of his tightly clenched eyelids, he could still see the swirling blue mist lazily raising over the Lake of Illusion. He could discern clearly the play and flicker of sound and image moving over the surface of the smooth glassy liquid. The mist continued to arrange and rearrange itself in ever changing, ever swirling hues of blue, shadows from the surface mixed with voices from the past, while all about, the air reeked of electrical discharge. It was as if the largest bolt of lightning imaginable had just exploded somewhere over the horizon, saturating the air with electrical energy.

He approached the lake slowly and with much trepidation. The mists rising from the flickering surface gathered in a large iridescent cloud which hovered above the lake like an immense mothership from an advanced civilization. Around the lake, nothing grew and nothing moved, except the incessant flickering from the surface. It was literally a broiling pool of idea manifest in image and sound. The composite dreams of humanity projected from within the lake itself upon its surface like a movie onto a screen. It was a psychic compost pile.

After awhile, Harry found that he could open his eyes against the brightness of the light. And though he was truly fascinated by the imagery and sound coming off the lake, he was smart enough to leave it alone and let it be. Without a moment's delay, and heeding Nth Degree's expert advice, he selected a stout log laying on the rocky beach and prepared to float across the Lake of Illusion upon his back. Just prior to pushing off, he plugged his ears with mud against the sounds of drama and intrigue that were rising with the mists and then, almost as an afterthought, he gathered a large handful of small stones, and laying back upon the log, pushed off across the lake. Almost immediately, he could hear the muffled cries and expectant whispers of illusory dream figures all about him. Keeping a lofty thought in mind, he carefully surrounded his body with a line of small stones and tried not to focus upon the ghostly images that were reflected up through the neon blue mists rising from the surface, like steam. A couple of times, he could see the shadows of large old sailing ships pass quite close to his small craft, but he never felt the ripple of their passing wake. A couple of other times, his hand accidentally trailed in the water, and as he glanced down, he almost became trapped within the unfolding watery drama that was being enacted below. The only thing that saved him were the stones, for whenever he would turn his head or move an arm or leg, the action would cause one of the stones to tumble into the lake, thus rippling the surface and spoiling the images momentarily, allowing him to free himself.

As Harry's little log boat floated on and on he grew tired and from time to time felt himself on the verge of falling asleep, which in his present position would have meant eternal slumber, for no one falls asleep crossing the Lake of Illusion without immediately becoming a character in the dreams of the deluded ones, for though the images flickering in the fog were very tenuous and ghost like, the pictures reflected upon the hard smooth surface of the lake were only too crystal clear. Indeed, they constituted a whole other reality, another entire zone of consciousness, and who was to cast the final vote as to which was the more real?

At one point, just before a stone tumbled into the dream fluid, one of the dream characters involved in some bit of soap opera-ish intrigue turned from the action and looked directly into Harry's eye, urgently beckoning him to join them beneath the surface. At that moment, had his hand not dislodged a stone, he would undoubtedly have joined them and thus become a prisoner within the lake, an entity trapped within the confines of another's dream.

When the character first turned and motioned to him, he felt that terminal sense of vertigo that often assails those who dare to peek behind the veil.

As he continued to drift through the fog, he kept his eyes directed upward and as unfocused as possible and reflected upon his life thus far. Some moments, he felt as if he were dreaming. Other moments, he felt as if he were being dreamed. He had the persistent feeling that there was something quite important which he was forgetting or blocking out. There were secrets here. Often, he could not even recall his reason for being and, within these moments, he saw himself as just another madman on the water, soon to be another stranger on the shore...serving as an interface or intraphase between illusion and delusion...too dense for space and obviously too spaced to matter.

But then, he would flush with embarrassment remembering that, deep below, somewhere within the catacombs of stone, a lonely creature by the name of *Nth Degree* scurried about looking after the well-being of those unhappy souls who had forgotten for a time that life was intended to be a prism and certainly not a prison. Reflecting thus, Harry soon felt much better and found himself, once again, able to keep his thoughts and goals aloft like large kites on a summer breeze. *Nth Degree, And, Sir Vain, Random Cause, General Havoc,* the wood chopper of *Happy Valley* and of course, *Desire* and his little monkey *Fascination* all floated above his mind's eye like outrageous personal attributes of

The Dreamer himself.

Harry's goals and desires were stressed, tested, refined and reaffirmed crossing the Lake of Illusion and any residual doubts soon evaporated like morning dew on a summer's day.

***

CHAPTER TWELVE

"Asher, the City of Light, and the Trapper of Wild Things"

Harry first caught sight of her peripherally, from the corner of his left eye. Starveling, pretty bones Indian girl in deer skin dress. She was tall and thin, and in her hands, she held a small clear bowl of dream liquid which she had just filled from the *Lake of Illusion*. She rose from the shore gracefully in preparation to lead Harry on. Within the small bowl, ideas and images darted around and about like tiny colorful fish. At first, he mistook her for a deer. She had that look and feeling about her: totally fearless and yet ready to spring and fling herself away at first sound or sudden movement. She was not like the other illusions he had witnessed floating across the lake. She was obviously very real, in fact, much more real than he was. She peered out of her large eyes like a great spiritual presence, peeking momentarily through a lens, into another, smaller world of creative interaction. Totally without prejudice, completely without judgement--"*just looking*", her expression seemed to confirm. Harry rolled over onto his stomach, as his log closed with the shore, and watched her, the Lake of Illusion suddenly forgotten. She was like a perimeter guard for an advanced race of beings who looked human, but were somehow para-human entities focused only temporarily within this dimension.

Around her waist, she wore a belt of whitish metal conches and whenever she turned, the light would catch and shoot off reflected beams in all directions. At that moment she was looking directly at Harry and one of the beams, reflected from her silvery belt, fell full upon his face. He could feel a small circle of warmth where he was touched by *the Light*.

"Are you an Angel?" he wondered, "I've heard of Angels."

She stood upon the shore slowly caressing her small bowl. Her eyes looked directly back into his. She smiled. "I'm an Angel with a broken wing," she seemed to say. And her lips never moved.

Waves of blissful feelings began to sweep over him like a narcotic, washing away the jungle grime of the imagination. He could feel himself being cleansed and burnished beneath her gaze. He felt himself being pulled toward her, like a fish caught upon a heavenly line. And this was only as it should be, for she was the mistress of ultimate compassion and her only desire was to fulfill the needs of others. She was called *Asher*.

As his log touched the shore, it took root, blossomed and threw off its seed, all before Harry's feet touched dry land. The Indian woman blinked her large dark eyes and within a twinkling, they both stood knee-deep in a field of white roses. For as far as he could see there were white roses standing like fields of wheat on a mid-western prairie. She casually picked one of the long-stemmed flowers and tossed it to him.

"Welcome to Paradise," her expression said with a simple smile.

Harry caught the flower with practiced precision as if his entire life had been mere preparation for this single exchange. She turned and began to move off across the field of white, cradling her bowl of human dreams in both hands like a precious object while he brought up the rear, holding the single rose before him like a magic wand, or a royal scepter. Soon the *Lake of Illusion* was a forgotten dream as together they moved through the fields of roses in search of the miraculous.

They traveled quickly and Harry was glad because the heady aroma from the flowers was about to make him ill. As they walked, the landscape appeared to slide beneath them effortlessly and yet it was obvious to him that his feet were on the ground because whenever he turned to look back over his shoulder, he saw his footprints following. He slid into *Paradise* as innocently as a child on a carnival ride, trusting and ever blissful across whole fields of ripening consciousness.

"I think I'm going to like this place," he thought to myself.

His guide turned and smiled. "You'll love it," she said with a wink. But of course her lips never moved, for in Paradise all is experienced directly and no thing is increased or made more meaningful by verbal comment.

It was here, in Paradise, that the souls, thawed from their icy confines deep within the caverns of Nth Degree, got to experience their most positive imaginings. It was in Paradise that the truly creative powers of human consciousness were finally freed beyond duality, to express as well as experience.

Asher continued forward, leading him on. They were beginning to move into the foothills and in the distance, Harry could see the beginnings of mountains. As they moved into the high country, they were treated to an ever-enlarging perspective as the worlds of *Paradise, Imagination, Content* and *Tranquility* spread out around them in all directions.

Soon they were in the mountains and the very fibers of Harry's inner ear began to reverberate with the sounds of music and yet no such sounds floated upon the air. As they moved along a path and up the side of one particularly rocky mountain face, he began to notice certain spots upon the rocks. These were strange transparent spots where the very surface of the rock had been worn away and become like a small clear window covered with downy pearlescent hairs. Asher informed him that these small hairs were in fact the chin whiskers belonging to a very rare breed of mountain goat which inhabited the area. The mountain, if not the entire area, Harry was led to believe, was of such a high order of idealized thought that the mere action of a goat, scratching its chin upon a rock, served to wear away the thin veneer of materiality and to reveal the innate transparency of the underlying concept.

And then, after what seemed to be days and days of trekking along goat paths in the high country, they rounded a rather steep precipice, and there, in the distance, stood buildings: signs of human habitation. To Harry, it appeared to be either a small city or else a very large village. Asher informed him that these were none other than the ivory towers of the *City of Light*. It stood in the distance, in a low valley surrounded by a perpetual snowfield. The city itself was as white as the purest snow is white, with many translucent domes, ivory towers, and streets of cobbled turquoise. The windows within the buildings seemed to be constructed of faceted opal and even the knobs upon the doors, it seemed to him, must surely be precious stones. Harry was truly moved as they drew closer for the total design of the town was so clean and precise that it literally sparkled and squeaked with clarity. It seemed to him so perfect, that the screws which held the separate concepts together must be diamonds and the hinges upon which the individual components swung would have had to be constructed of the purest Eastern jade. According to Asher, this was the *City of Light*, the *Crystal City*, which lay securely centered within the core of the Earth, like an exquisitely crafted watch in the hand of God. The citizens of this place were the first sons and daughters of *The Dreamer* who had moved beyond the pale.

Harry was aglow with sudden desire! He immediately grabbed his flute and wanted to enter the city and play his music for the citizens, in the style of a traveling minstrel, but one admonishing glance from Asher was enough to cool his ardor. This place was far beyond the realm of mere desire, her mind seemed to say to his. And human goals, no matter how lofty, were best checked at the edge of the *Lake of Illusion*, like a dusty cloak at the door of a very special house. But why, he wondered, was he even given this view of the *Crystal City*?

Well, she seemed to reply, perhaps, it has been found in the past, it helps idealistic young questors to know of such a place. It seems to sooth and console them when they find themselves stuck and all alone in some outback of peripheral consciousness. It is comforting, when lost, a thousand years from nowhere, in the darkness and the black, to recall that somewhere in the high country, there is a place so conscious that it actually glitters with the many faceted light of twinkling realization.

Harry nodded as if to himself. But what do they do, he wondered? What is it that makes them so different from the rest of us?

Asher looked from his face back toward the city-glow in the distance. "They have no questions and are in search of no answers. They are neither for, nor against, and they do not explain themselves, for they hate good sense..." And her lips never moved and no sound floated upon the air.

It was only with the greatest reluctance that he let himself be led along a circuitous route which skirted the crystal city and eventually brought them out onto a wide flat plateau. Behind them loomed the huge mountain with its secret place, while before them, beyond the plateau, stretched a wide lush valley. At the very center of the rocky shelf sat two round stones, and between the stones was a hole in the ground from which rose warm fragrant vapors that turned to steam as they lazily trailed upwards into the sky. Harry learned from his Angel that this was the place of sitting together. Asher sat on one side of this strange vent from the inner world and motioned for Harry to seat himself on the other side. As soon as they were both seated on the stones facing one another, the angel with the broken wing, as she referred to herself, placed her container of human dreams over the hole in the ground and then removed her hands. The small bowl of multicolored forms hovered in the air above the opening, turning slowly like a balloon riding a column of air. Asher looked directly into Harry's eyes and held out her hands. Without uttering a sound or thinking a thought, Harry extended his arms, one on either side of the floating bowl. The rock seats were situated so that with arms extended only the very tips of their fingers touched. As he touched her skin he was shot through with a sensation of utter and absolute peace. His body sagged slightly as if a great weight had been removed from his shoulders. It was as if his head had somehow been most pleasantly removed from the bulk of his body and allowed to float free between them at the place of sitting together, exactly like the small bowl of human dreams. The being that faced him was graced with such an expression of utter poise and contentment that he felt himself begin to flow into her and he felt her begin to flow through him and though it felt as if tears of gratitude trailed from his eyes, he knew there was no trace of moisture upon his face.

Soon their intertwining entities succeeded in creating a unified pool of being and upon the surface of this pool there was not the slightest ripple. All thought, all reflection, all recording, all processing ceased. Like twin stars orbiting a black hole in deepest space they moved, circling slowly, and then more rapidly around the center of gravity that hovered between them like a point of celestial punctuation. They soon accelerated to such a level that for all intents and purposes they appeared to be absolutely still, a mere point of light on an otherwise moonless night. Together they constituted an invisible stitch in a seamless garment. Their extended fingers continued to brush against one another like eyelashes tracing the subtle undulations of earth itself while in the center, between them, the small, slowly revolving bowl of human dreams was beginning to empty.

"Yep! That's what I said! Three days out. Only three days. Do you hear me?"

She eyed him gently with compassion, like a once beautiful woman viewing herself in an early morning mirror.

"There were twelve of us left by then and we had four years worth of pelts. A fortune, honey! And it 'twas then that they hit us! Must o' been at least twenty of the filthy heathens. Before I knew it, all hell broke loose. Screamin', shootin'! Never heard such screamin' and carryin' on, and the pain! The pain...oh, my gawd, the pain..."

"Let it go. Let it pass through. Don't try to hold it," she seemed to say.

"One of them injuns got me with his axe right here..."

Harry held up the better half of his left arm. "Just as I was getting up--CRACK! Never heard such a sound before. I heard the bone snap and I fell and rolled down the hill into a dry creek bed. Well, pretty soon I opened my eyes and everything was very quiet. There weren't no sound--exceptin' the dry rattle of my own breath in my chest like a mournful wind..."

He sat with his arms extended like a healthy tree, feeling as if he had just oozed into material form. He was one side, she was the other. Above them both, the steamy vapors from the center of the earth mingled with the steamy vapors of one man's dream.

"So, do you know what I did then?"

Harry was now a trapper, a hunter of skins from beyond the big sea. He sat somewhere in ancient Califia, in a frontier town, in a saloon telling stories and drinking with a half-breed barmaid. As he talked, she kept filling and refilling his extended glass with strong drink. The bar was crowded and quite loud, causing him to shout at his companion, his woman for the night. She sat quietly, passively watching this creature dream his man dream.

"No," her eyes seemed to say, "what did you do then?"

"Hell, woman! I'll tell you what I did, I didn't do no thing!" At this point his husky voice erupted in laughter. "Them injuns are slick little devils. I knew they was just watchin' and waitin' for me to make a noise, so they could come find me and take off the top o' my head. So I laid there and played dead for three days in that dusty ol' creek with nothing to keep me alive but a pee-trickle of water oozing from between two rocks. Finally, the damn pain and infection got so bad I had to cut off the rest o' my arm with my skinnin' knife. Just got it off too when I heard--the horse! Jesus, I thought, here they come. I'm a dead man for sure...I was scared, I'm not ashamed to say. So I crawled real careful like through the bush and what do you think I saw?"

The woman refilled his glass. "What did you see?" her mind seemed to inquire of his.

"Well..." said the killer of animals and the collector of skins, "I'll tell you what I saw...another trapper! Just like my very own self. Can you beat that? A mountain man nosin' around among the bodies lookin' for stuff! What luck I says to my own self. Counted myself for dead and here is a horse delivered up right nice, too. So, to show my, ah, appreciation, I killed him real quick and neat. I slipped the point o' my skinnin' knife in under his left ear as he was stooped over going through the pockets of one o' my dead partners."

Suddenly the trapper lapsed into a hacking laugh that degenerated into a tubercular cough. "Never even squealed! Just fell like a stuck hog. So, here I am, ha-ha-ha!"

The woman looked at him with just the slightest trace of a smile on her face. "So here you are," her expression seemed to say.

Harry looked into her eyes for the first time and dropped his glass. The simple truth of her expression struck him like a shot and like a victim he fell.

.

He fell from the rim of a cliff at the dawn of the age of warm-blooded creatures. He fell to the ground, victim of an adversary's arrow. He fell from the back of a galloping horse in the Middle Ages and suffocated within the confines of his own armor, drowning in his own blood. He fell from the belly of a burning aircraft and he was flushed from the belly of another with a high pressure hose. He fell victim to countless assassins' bullets and he fell to the ground and covered his eyes to no avail when he saw the great burst of light in the Western sky. He fell victim to countless plagues and generations of illness both physical as well as mental. He fell in all the ways that it is imaginable for a man creature to fall. He fell victim to greed and temptation and envy and hatred and resentment and sloth and anger.

His entire existence suddenly appeared to be a close study into the nature of the falling phenomenon. He seemed to wake up only to fall asleep, and he seemed to stand up only to fall down. And each and every time, at the moment of the hit, he would wonder, how many more times do I have to go through this?

***

Honeysuckle, lavender, delta calm.
Like the dark stone heart of some unbearably ancient thing:
A woman, a cage of tears, a ferny day.
"I'll catch you yet, lady of luck, 'cause
I've baited my hook with Light".
Starveling child, changeling, pretty bones
Indian girl in a deer skin dress.
"Are you an Angel? I've heard of Angels, I believe in Angels"
"Asher is my name," she seemed to say,
with the merest hint of a smile.
"I'm an Angel with a broken wing"

***

CHAPTER THIRTEEN

"A Pretender in Paradise"

"Wake up! Wake up! Wake up, you wastrel!"

Harry opened his eyes slowly to the noisy din. He seemed to be laying on a floor in a room crowded with awesome foul-smelling creatures. Now, as his eyes adjusted to the torchlit twilight, he could see that his head was laying on a table and apparently there was some sort of celebration going on. All about him strange, longhaired humanoid creatures were making great loud noises attempting to rouse him into consciousness. They had an accent, a dialect, almost a brogue. He found their speech pattern familiar and yet hard to place. Each and every syllable had the metallic clink of a small coin dropped onto a hard marble surface.

"Wake up! You can't be here! What are you doing in this hallowed place?"

None of this made much sense to him at the time. He raised his head off the long slab of wood and tried to sort through the mass of tangled thoughts that crowded his mind. He felt like a fisherman with a bad backlash. He was apparently at some sort of primitive feast and, where was Asher?

"You shouldn't really be here, you know?" said a friendly voice close to his head.

"*REALLY*!" said an exaggerated male voice with great indignation from across the table.

"Pass the wine and bust 'is head!" said another.

"Out with the bastid'!"

"A pretender, for sure," commented yet another.

Suddenly, Harry felt someone nudge him in the side. It was the friendly voice. He looked to his left and a dour-looking manbeast creature with leather breasts and a great horned helmet pushed a silver flagon of wine into his hand.

"Go ahead, boy. Put Christmas in your eyes, keep your voice low and speak of Paradise, and see where it gets you, ha-ha-ha!"

"He's a fraud! He don't belong here. Heave him out!" screamed a loud voice from far down the table.

"Yeah! This is a hero's hall. We're all heroes here and he just don't belong."

"Hold on now. Hold on." cried a deep rich authoritative voice. "He's a fraud for sure and he don't belong here, for certain, but he's still a hero, only he don't know it yet. I say every man, woman and child that's ever put on skin and walked this green and sacred globe is a hero!"

"A hero, each and ever one!"

"Aye!" said another gravely

"Here, here," cried the group as a whole, raising their silver chalices, "Three cheers for mankind!"

"But to be a true hero, one's got to know he's a hero. How one handles that knowledge, that's what makes him a hero!"

"Aye, and I say 'cause he ain't realized it yet, he ain't no hero--he's just another pretender."

"Yeah, just another flat spot on the wheel..."

So here they were, the warriors, the victors and the victims, the killers and the killed, who, having died gloriously in battle, were sharing a last feast in *Valhalla*. They sat around the table like personified violence. Horned steel and silver helmets, encrusted with precious stones, and shields and flags, heavy with clan symbols, hung from the walls along with swords and knives and daggers and bloody battle axes. There were at least fifty of them circling the entire table; hairy with muscles stacked like thick steaks beneath a shoplifter's coat. There was Cumin and Turmeric and Cardamon and his brother, Fenugreek, and all the rest too numerous to mention and, of course, the leader, the lord of this celebration, Coriander.

Suddenly there came a great crash from the head of the table as a goodly portion of the long wooden slab exploded into splinters and pulp.

"*Who is this CREATURE!*" cried the great Coriander, smashing his short broad sword into the once living oak.

In the ensuing silence, all eyes turned slowly in Harry's direction.

A friendly face to his left inquired politely, "Friend, how did thou get here without the traditional garments of a true Viking lord?"

"Well...ahh" Harry began, trying to voice a suitable response, but the words just bubbled uselessly in his throat.

"Well...?" said an isolated voice from somewhere down the line, "if you can't see it from wisdom, then you must obviously be forced to live, or die, through the experience!"

"How true...how true." responded yet another.

"*SILENCE!*" bellowed King Coriander from his position at the head of the table. "*BIND THIS MAN HAND AND FOOT AND CAST HIM INTO THE OUTER DARKNESS!*"

"But, sir..." Harry sputtered, trying to explain his way out of this most difficult situation. "I'm just a tourist. I really don't belong here, don't you see. I'm just passing through. This is just...*practice.*"

"*PASSING THROUGH*!" cried Coriander, "*PRACTICE*! What blasphemy. Practice, indeed. Seize this, this person, this hu-man and cast him and his hu-man desire into the outer darkness!"

The sentence had scarcely been uttered when the entire warrior horde began to descend upon Harry as if he were a bag of garbage and it was collection day. He stood, panic stricken, and retreated to the door as the paradisal forms advanced. As they closed with him, ropes and weapons in hand, he reached for the door and found it quick to open at his touch. He turned and ran into a wall of night, pursued by anonymous voices. He ran and ran, until he could run no further, and when he could no longer run, he walked fast, and when even that became too much of an effort, then he walked slow until rested, at which time he would resume running again. He ran with nothing but his pipe and his pouch and his red wooden flute. He ran because he knew that he was a pretender in Paradise. He felt certain that the Viking horde would not really harm him, but he also knew that this was their Paradise and not his. The longer he ran the more confident he became that by this action he would be led eventually to find his own particular vision of Paradise.

In the distance, Harry saw lights on the horizon and as he drew closer, he saw that these were small fires and sitting around these fires were ragged- looking men with tattered clothes and scraggly beards. These he discovered were the hobo's of Heaven, crouching about their campfires at the base of the Rock Candy Mountain, drinking from a whisky stream and eating from a pool of hearty stew. These were the ones, who, in life, made the tragic mistake of becoming professional humans. These were the work-obsessed, taking advantage, now, of the freedom offered in Paradise. Harry stopped for a while to listen as they swapped lies and spoke of their earthly adventures, exchanging pieces of paper and cutting deals. Now they shared the great, good comradeship that was denied them in life. Soon though, they admonished him to move on, least they, too, join the crowd and pursue him to the very edge. For they, too, could tell at a glance that Harry did not belong in Paradise. And so, with the sounds of the Vikings growing ever closer, he turned to run once again. As the cycles of running, jogging and walking continued on and on and on, only to be replaced one by the other, he became gradually aware of a growing lightness on the horizon. The darkness was retreating, and soon it was to be the dawn of a new day.

Through the course of his long dark night he had left the mountains and the foothills, and had crossed the wide grassy plain which, with the light, had become a hard flat rocky ground. Now that the light was in the sky and his pursuers were far behind, he found himself standing, incredulous, at the very edge of a sudden and apparently bottomless abyss. He ran along the edge of the great break, first in one direction and then in the other, looking for a passage, a natural bridge over which he might quickly pass. There was no bridge. Nor was there any natural substance: wood, reed, or rope with which to fashion a point of passage. He sat down upon the very edge and reflected upon his rather grave situation. He felt trapped by his frustrations. He felt like a cat on a blackboard with claws engaged futilely trying to rise above himself. Though the break was only about twenty feet wide, it appeared to be bottomless and he dared not risk a running jump, for if he should fail...he would surely spend the rest of eternity experiencing the phenomena of falling. How deep was it, he wondered, and what lay at the very bottom? He scooted close to the edge and pushed over a small rock. He watched as it was quickly swallowed up by the darkness of the abyss and then he listened for its report, but the sound never came. He felt saddened; to have come so far only to be caught, trapped by a crack in the earth.

At that very moment, Harry's eye caught a movement in the

distance, on the far side of the break in the ground. Approaching across the barren prairie of mind ground was a large cream-colored horse and riding atop the beast was what appeared to be a young woman with long yellow hair that trailed out behind her in the wind as she rode. He watched her intently as she approached, for she seemed to take a most indirect route. She moved back and forth in the distance, as if she were approaching over a stream, jumping from rock to rock, negotiating a most difficult course in order to reach him.

***

CHAPTER FOURTEEN

"Faith, Speculation and The Bridge"

"Well!" she laughed as she drew close to the edge. "Looks like you've reached the edge of a rather large idea, luv, haven't you?"

Harry stared at her. She, too, had the habit, like Asher, of speaking without moving her lips. She appeared quite young, younger than he and she seemed to float, rather than ride, a couple of inches immediately above the beast's broad back. And whenever she would look directly at him there seemed to be a diffused beam of multicolored light that poured from her eyes. She was continually moving, but not so much from nervousness or restlessness; it was more, it was as if she were weaving some sort of pattern or invisible web with her apparently random motions.

"Shame, shame!" she directed at Harry as if she were enjoying some sport at his expense. "Whatever will you think of now, luv," she laughed as she moved along, atop her beautiful palomino, continuing her intricate dance of unknown significance. "But," she continued, shooting him a meaningful sidelong glance, "don't stop to drop upon a once-remembered time. Travel through your thoughts rapidly and your compass will not waver."

Harry stood at the edge. He wanted to cross; he told her so. She told him there was no problem. He said that it was obviously too far to jump. She advised him to build a bridge. He looked around desperately, fearing approaching noises from the rear and told her that his search had proved fruitless; He had found nothing with which to construct a bridge. What could he use?

She laughed again, sounding somehow like a vain angel engrossed in the act of brushing her hair. "Use your mind, luv! That's what got you here and I dare say, in the end, that's what will have to get you out, one way or the other." And then her mood became more serious. "You are not what you have been told, luv," she said looking directly at him with her great fly's eyes pouring out light. "When thought and experience become one, reality is changed. Fill the gap in your expanding consciousness with faith, luv, and not doubt! Allow awareness to find you! Link up with the Dreamer and find the harmony bridge! Let your thought become the experience."

He watched her seated high on her horse, on the far side of the abyss. He had never encountered such a strange creature in all of his travels. "I just don't understand," he said. "I guess I'm just dumb as well as ignorant."

"No!" she said swirling around in a tight circle, throwing off sparks of light. "You're not ignorant, you're just forgetful, luv, that's all. With harmony will come the vision."

" But," he said, "what's there?"

"What's where?" she replied, all silvery and cool, like a mountain stream.

"What's down there?" he said, pushing over another small stone into the abyss. "Down there, at the very bottom?"

"Oh," she replied casually, "just stray thoughts, third-rate passions and prejudices.

"It's like peeling an onion in reverse," she continued. "You must think it through, layer at a time. When you have conceived of enough layers, then merely witness the reality. Let your rescue ropes be woven of synchronicity."

Harry looked at her. "I have no idea what you are talking about."

"Plain and simple, luv, you have to create a bridge with your imagination, within your mind! It's all a matter of symbolism. Even we are but mere symbols for our very active minds."

Harry just looked at her and then down into the primeval darkness and shook his head.

"Any external aide like wood or rope would be merely metaphorical substitutes for your internal doubt. After all, luv, the greatest physical monuments in the entire world are merely testimony to man's basic doubt. Why build a towering structure to your lack of faith; skip it! Literally!"

"But what do I do, specifically?" he asked. "What can I do? I can't help it if my mind doubts?"

She looked directly at him and the light from her eyes seemed to pour over the edge of the abyss like small round luminous balls of fire that exploded seconds later in the depths. "Time to move beyond, luv. Mind does not doubt, brain is the doubt! Go beyond your brain. It is not needed, now."

As Harry watched, she stood up on her mount's back, with her long yellow hair trailing down like a fine suit of silken gold and began to turn in a circle. Faster and tighter she began to spin, until she became as a pinwheel of brilliant light, sending off a shower of sparks, some of which flew completely over the abyss.

"You see," she said with an almost human smile. "All matter is merely trapped light, *light is life*! Look upon your brain, luv, as merely a focusing device, so that you might be better able to focus, and thus construct specific events within...time. This will enable you to access your larger Mind."

Harry glanced down at the tiny sparks from her *Being* that clung to his rough clothes like droplets of water on oil cloth. As he watched, the individual drops would cling for a second or two, and then abruptly dart off as living things, lightning bugs, and fire flies. It was a sight to behold and he felt, if not transformed, at least uplifted.

"What are these events in time called?" he inquired.

"Well," she replied, resuming a more natural position upon the back of her palomino and hunching forward in his direction. "If the intent is pure and if the event inspires the quiet place that lies within...then it is often called, *art*."

"*Art,* is it?" he responded, turning the concept over within his mind's frame. "And, if the intent is not so pure and the event created somehow fails to inspire? What is it called then?"

"If it is sincerely honored by an awkward spirit, then it is still art, and if not, well, then..." she insinuated with a flick of her finger and a shrug of her shoulders, "it is just more dust upon the wheel, another crowded place upon the road. You see, luv, entities are very transitory, they're forever changing and transforming themselves into one thing or another. Life is a butterfly on the wind of creation. We are born, we stretch our color beneath the sun, and flutter about for a day and we are gone. *POOF*! Off to become other things in other places. Whereas, art, created by these same entities, lingers about and long outlives the temporal form of its creator and forms of itself a silent chain down through the corridors of time that parodies the stiff and formal antics of mere politicians, generals and other would-be shapers of this three-dimensional world. These events in time, luv, are dream drops and spirit spoor. They attest to the fact that the Dreamer has wandered this road."

Harry was agitated. He was afraid and he admitted it. "I find myself chased to the very edge and forced to create a bridge. I find myself doubting that such a thing can even be done. I don't see why you even bothered to bring up the matter..."

She laughed good naturedly, as her steed moved restlessly sideways along the edge of the abyss. "I see you not only for who you are, Harry, but also for who you have been and who you are to become. You are an artist, whose task it is to create events in time, and though you may not be able to fathom the awesome depth of the *Big Sea*, you certainly can create your own rainbow!" And as she spoke, she made a grand gesture with her left arm, creating a brilliant seven-color rainbow, spanning the gorge of fear that Harry chose to look upon as his abyss.

"Or," she uttered with another grand sweep of her delicate hand, "you may choose to condense it down to a more solid form suitable for walking upon." And as the ground trembled, the diffuse red, orange, yellow, green, blue, indigo, and violet of the rainbow began to condense down, down, down until the very idea became a most substantial, though ethereal looking sparkling bridge, suitable perhaps for walking upon. "As you can see," she gestured with a smile, "there are many ways to bring up *the matter*, as you say."

"But," he inquired once again. "What is *down* there?"

"Nothing but the thinking brain," replied the lady and without a moment's hesitation, she stepped out over the edge of the abyss, riding high upon the back of her pale yellow horse. "There is the world of doing and the world of being," she said, "if running become the running and not the runner. *I am the bridge*!"

As Harry watched open-mouthed and transfixed, she rode her horse over the edge and across the pastel purple and pearlescent bridge, like a grand idea whose time had come

.

"All life is light, Harry!" she said at mid-span, "All consciousness manifests itself as light; light chasing itself in a divine dance. Matter is merely gravitationally-trapped light. The *'jump'* must occur at a speed faster than that of light. It is that simple!"

As she approached his side of the abyss, she said, "Remember, luv, a blind man does not live in darkness...think of your mind as a rope spanning an abyss between body and soul and walk across that rope with perfect confidence, because that's what you are here for."

But, as her horse's hooves touched the near side of the fathomless abyss, the pastel-colored bridgeness lingered for only a moment, before it began to evaporate like a string of bubbles in a glass of carbonated water. As the bridge disappeared, his vision slid once again into the abyss.

"Your brain is merely a lens, Harry, a focusing device used by your Mind. Now focus on your bridge as having been and then merely slide it into the present." she said. "It's all a matter of focus, I can assure you."

"But what is really down there?" he exclaimed pointing down into the blackness. "I must know!"

"Broken hearts and shattered dreams," she replied without a moment's hesitation.

"Oh, I just don't know," he cried, looking up at the young woman. "I just don't know. I can't do that!" He said referring to the bridge that he had just observed. "And besides, why do I have to go across? After all, Paradise is not such a bad place to be and I'm sure that those who pursue me really intend me no harm. Is it not true that all is Paradise?"

"This is true. This is, after all, your story, luv. You can create or change whatever it is that you might want to create or change. You are the author of your own reality. There is no one over you, Harry. But now, you must cross. No matter what happens, you must go and grow and increase your conscious awareness by fulfilling those certain specific values which you hold to be important. So you believe, and so it will be done, behind the doors of your perception, if necessary. This may be paradise, luv, but it is not your Paradise. *True Paradise* is created, not merely discovered."

"But what is down there--**DEATH**?" He pleaded.

"Slow down, luv. You are going too fast." she said in soothing tones. "Become like the earth. Stay in sync. Allow your thinking brain to simply fall away and link your being with the real Dreamer of this moment."

Harry looked at her seated beside him on her high horse and together they imagined and so it was that they were eventually able to establish a certain harmony between the general and the specific; between the "*might be--could be*" and the "*should be-has to be.*" And when she had energized him to the point where he, too, could see the very reason for being, then and only then did she lean slowly over her pale horse's shoulder and touch him gently upon his head with her right hand. At that very instant, it suddenly became very clear for Harry. It became as clear as the finest glass, mind-blown across a gorge of seemingly infinite fear and forgetfulness. High arching strands of emerald green and substantial ridges of the deepest purple, held together with diamond screws and bound and wrapped with golden rope.

"Jump!" she whispered into the right side of his head. "Leap..."

And so, like a lunatic striding across the Grand Canyon on an unseen filament of spider stuff, Harry stepped out away from the edge of one idea and onto the structural relevance of another. He strutted out across the unseen toward the unknown performing the oldest dance known to man. His goal was to grasp the light, to capture it, and release it, without getting burned. He wanted to surf the curve of binding energy and this wave was his. He wanted to ride into the flame, along the edge of the sword, and emerge reborn. This was why he had come here. This was why he had become a questor. He wanted to have a dream and live it too. This was why he had become a hu-man. Like a comedic actor in an old time silent movie, he strobed across the abyss, leaving a filmy pearlescent trail of wispy but real bridgeness.

"Remember, luv," she called after him in a whimsical tone, "you're not ignorant, just forgetful."

It was at that point, that Harry discovered that though he was, indeed, slow, and though his spiritual muscles were weak from habitual sloth and disuse and doubt, still it all began to fall rapidly into place and instincts and abilities dormant for untold lifetimes suddenly came to him without effort, as if they had been his--always! His muscles soon became an extension of his will; his body became the brush with which his mind illustrated its intent upon this earth. And as the transformation became complete Harry realized that he was not an animal trapped in the traces of habit like a beast in a field. He began to realize that he was indeed a free creative spirit! He was a direct descendant of *The Dreamer*. He was an orphaned heir taking yet another step on the long journey back home. He was an open-ended consciousness; there were no limitations! Thus Harry moved on the merest thread of self-generated thought, confident in the strength of this--the integrity of the moment. He felt as if he were drawing together two disparate seams of time. During these moments, his faith was strong enough to enable him to linger awhile at point balance of a sigh and witness the miraculous act of a physical body, materialized in time and space, standing atop a bridge of pure imagination, which would soon enough began to fade and finally evaporate like earthly beauty into the ethereal vapors.

As Harry crossed to the other side, he turned and with his newly charged state of consciousness, saw the young female creature with the yellow hair and her palomino horse as an incredible whirling light throwing off sparks which popped and sizzled in all directions.

"Well, now," she seemed to say, "look at this--the power and the creativity we call Harry! Look at you. Like a true son of Adam, driven from Paradise, a child at heart reliving once again the first day of creation!" She turned and wheeled her horse back up on its two legs, sending off an astounding display of color and light. "You are now part of a wave, luv..." she told him. "You are now part of the leading edge of *The New Dawn*, holding on the horizon about to break upon the world!"

Harry simply stood on the opposite edge of the great abyss, breathing in and breathing out.

"Off with you now, luv," she gestured with a flick of her wrists. "Run off and make all things new again. Go on now and do whatever it is that you have to do and you needn't worry, we will meet again, luv."

Harry turned to leave and then turned back again. They looked upon each other across the chasm for a long while. Finally he spoke. "It's been a real pleasure," he said.

The young lady smiled sincerely and waved and the movement of her arm somehow caused reality to pucker and shimmer, leaving a ghostly trail of after-images. "It's always a pleasure, Harry," she said.

He smiled and then after a moment of silence he felt impelled to ask. "Who are you? What do they call you?"

She laughed as her horse moved restlessly along the edge, and her melodious tones fell across the abyss like notes from a harp strung with angel hair

.

"Think of me merely as *Faith*," she called. "I am the lone rider, the one who rides along the very edge, with my wild stallion called *Speculation*." She laughed again. "Now fly, my little eaglet, and give my best to those in high places."

As Faith rode off into the distance, lesser lights approached over the hard rocky ground and, as they closed with the very edge of the abyss, they became less bright and their radiance transformed itself into fleshy reality--Viking reality. They stood about, suddenly happy, all smiling and shooting off grins like sparks from side to side. Like an ethereal wheel that having rolled up, suddenly separates itself into individual spokes: there was Cardamon and Cumin and Fenugreek and shy Turmeric and in the background were even a couple of the hobos that Harry had encountered by their fires at the base of Rock Candy Mountain. But, of course, it was Coriander who laughed the loudest, for he was indeed pleased that Harry had succeeded in finding his way across the big divide and could now continue his journey which would hopefully lead him eventually to his own version of Paradise.

Harry laughed, too, and said that he hoped that they weren't still there feasting when he returned one day. They all laughed again by way of parting and slowly moved back away from the edge, shouting the time-honored form of both greeting and farewell in Paradise. *"Light is life!"*

"Light is life!" Harry echoed.

***

CHAPTER FIFTEEN

"The Time Travelers, the Standing Dead, and the White Dolphin"

Harry felt still and delicious. All his friends had moved away again and he turned toward the future feeling mellow and open and fluid. He walked for a long while across the vast prairie of Mind Ground that lay on the far side of the abyss. He traveled for days and days, plodding through the short grass and sleeping in small depressions to escape the terrible wind. During his waking hours he would blow his desire through the finely holed piece of red bamboo that he carried always at his side, along with his pouch and his pipe. As he played he would try to imagine the sea and the white dolphin that would lead him to the source, to the *Dreamer of All That Is.*

After many, many hours, the self-conscious whistles and squeaks which he made upon his instrument became more and more melodious. Gradually, after many, many days of practice, his sound became transformed: it became musical...soulful, in fact.

During these long slow days and nights, Harry saw no one nor any living thing. Since crossing the abyss, he had given up wishing and fantasizing about the source of this dream he called his life, his quest. He merely walked along, watching the light, and breathing in and breathing out. When he became tired he would simply sit and rest and play his flute. When he became sleepy, he would recline and fold his body into one of the many shallow craters that dotted the grassy landscape and close his eyes. His mind was peaceful. It was easy. Harry's life was simple. He neither hungered nor thirsted. He was now beyond desire. He blew it away each morning upon arising. He felt full and accomplished, like a rock...or a streak of light.

One day as Harry sat, motionless, drifting with the stellar flux, he saw a large flight of small black birds. They seemed to arrive with the afternoon wind: at least five hundred of them, harvesting seeds from the fields. As he watched they swooped and zoomed through the air like one huge wing. They would climb high and then drop in massive elegance over the fields of short grass. Incredible and beautiful, they moved as one animal. They would sweep and fold and reverse direction, never bunching up, always in perfect position. The five hundred separate bird bodies were like individual knots that connected an otherwise invisible net thrown by an unseen hand.

In salute to the first living things he had seen in a long while, Harry lifted his instrument to his lips and began to blow. As he blew his intention through the bamboo tube, he distinctly heard a low whistle somewhere in the distance. At first, he assumed that it must be some sort of sympathetic echo from the flight of black birds, but then, as he continued to play, the accompanying whistle grew louder. Turning, he casually observed a small cloud forming on the distant horizon. As he watched, the growing cloud gradually began to condense and move. The low whistle in the distance was coming from the cloud. It slowly began to tighten and turn, approaching over the grassy prairie like a golden fire. At first it was quite slow and graceful, like a drop of milk in a glass of water, but then it began to turn faster and faster as it grew larger, tightening into a massive cyclonic form of mythic proportions. Harry quickly stood and began to move off towards the right in hopes of evading it--whatever it was. But as he ran, the approaching cyclonic form tightened its focus and moved towards the right. Harry quickly reversed his direction and doubled his speed, but still the cyclone followed, moving over the prairie of barren Mind Ground like a predatory animal that had his scent and was intent upon a kill. As its approach and eventual interception grew eminent, Harry sat down upon the ground and attempted to gather his stray thoughts about him and prepare himself for the future. Once he was centered and his fears were accounted for he gathered his powers of concentration about him like a secure cloak in the face of an onrushing storm--for one thing, at least was certain, and that was the meeting between the approaching force that appeared to be plotting its own course and Harry--whose direction, whose very life was about to be suddenly and irrevocably altered.

He slowly picked up his instrument. It felt like he was about to blow his life through its tiny narrow channels, for the magnitude of the onrushing wave of cyclonic activity, which now stretched from one edge of his mind's sight to the other, was about to make short work of his physical body.

The gentle, initially-inspiring, low whistle had now grown into an awesome scream, as if all creation were contained within the cloud tower trying desperately to escape. The combined struggle seemed to give the white mass its whorling spin, like the most incredibly dense thought ever conceived within the mind of The Muse, turning back upon itself in appreciation of its own magnitude. As Harry recalled his one-time experience with the rather awesome Phoenix, it now seemed as a tamed bird in a gilded cage. He tried to take solace in some advice given him long ago by a wonderful little old man called *And*.

"When you are going up or coming down, you are vulnerable, the window is open. When the elevator is moving there are no doors between floors. The blast of reality will blow right through. Sometimes it will blow right through you and other times it will blow you right through--to the other side of the maze..."

Harry's first impression was of light-sparks reverberating through the tight moist warmness of his fingers as they continued to grasp the wooden fibers of the flute. And then the delirious skies opened for this wanderer, and it was on him and over him in an instant. The dense heat of the idea seemed to split his teeth in sections like lead fragments spent from the tube of a smoldering gun, while the rising odor of burnt sulfur began to waft through his skull, reminding his butterfly brain that it was time to be reborn. Faster and faster and faster he began to spin. Faster and faster and with each revolution, Harry began to rise, faster than the speed of light, faster even than the speed of Mind, he began to weep, to reap the laughter and the gift that is consciousness.

It was a weighty experience; suddenly LIFE itself was lifting him to her craggy bosom and above the tops of the rolling waves a rich feminine voice began to speak and this is what it seemed to say..."I'm speaking to you, love, from the essence of what is true, love; infinity is yours, laid before you. You have feet as a base from which to view the infinite as it spreads before you in all directions with you as a center. It is made meaningful by desire and relevant through the freedom of choice. You have eyes from which to reflect love to all things. You have imagination as your crystal and you have an ego in which to hold it. By only trusting, you can have eternal realization..."

Harry was exhausted. He felt like a wet sheet blowing in a polluted breeze. He was giddy. He felt like laughing. He laughed. He felt he could record the color and odor found within any specific room in space. His mind was reduced to a piece of litmus paper. He found himself testing for cosmic acidity. These anxious bits and pieces of human thought zipped and darted around and about within his mind like tropical fish in a closed tank at feeding time. Or like electrons and protons in a cloud chamber, these bits and pieces of insight cried out their message and left a smoky trail to mark their passing. Unfortunately, this specific cloud chamber must have been located in an American University and it must have been the lunch hour, for there was obviously nobody paying attention--no eyes other than Harry's to watch and be astonished at the series of random impulses spelling out patterns, which in turn twisted themselves helix-like into individual letters, which in turn grouped as words and as words found themselves attracted to other words, which gave want to feeling and feeling to phrase and phrase to metaphorical innuendo.

Harry looked upward and beheld a great machine, a great cloud of fire enfolding itself with a brightness about it and out of the midst came the likeness of four living creatures. They had the likeness of a man but every one had four faces and each one had four wings. Their appearance was like burning coals of fire and their appearance was of lamps. The light traveled down among the creatures and it was bright and it moved back and forth like slow lightning. And when Harry heard the noise of their wings, it was like the noise of great waters, like the noise of speech. And there was a brightness around and about them like a rainbow.

The leader told Harry to stand on a specific three foot section of the metal floor. As he did, the small square of metal began to drop, lowering him into a room below. Protruding from the floor of this second room were the top portions of three globes he had observed under the belly of the huge craft as it approached. The globes were transparent and contained what seemed to be large diamonds or crystals. On each side of every crystal were rods which sloped inward. He asked the leader to explain how this propulsion system worked. The leader replied with a subtle smile, "Don't even try to understand it." But then he seemed to soften and add, almost as an afterthought, "But with just a little more thought on your own, this could be developed by your people."

"Where are you from?" Harry asked. "Which distant star or planet do you call home?"

The creature smiled again, "This is home. We are your elders from a gentler time in space. We travel through time as you travel through water. We are from earth, my friend. We are the same as you. In fact, in a very real sense, we are you. Think of us as a future extension of yourself, as we see you as a past projection of ourselves."

The Star Creature, for this was how he referred to himself, said that his essence came from the heart of the Sun and he made Harry realize that he was not discovering "*the way it was,*" he was not discovering anything. He was creating "*the way it is.*" He was part of a slowly spinning cloud of idea which was the very opposite of the abyss. He was caught up in the ultimate in focus which was engaged in sucking up energy from the *Mind Ground* in order to feed its central mystery. He was made aware that the whole of the earth with all of its flora, fauna, male and female, is but a conscious work of art, and the subtle inner tracings within the mind of man is nothing less than the gradual awakening of a fledgling artist growing through time and space and the experience of creation. Humans are creators, shapers, it would seem, suffering the pangs of birth.

The Star Creature pointed down to a shiny thing; a smooth flat glassy reflective screen. Harry moved closer to see what it was that was reflected within its surface, but he was only able to catch a quick glimpse before the Star Creatures put him down again in the grassy field. From what he saw on the screen, it had appeared to be merely an old man dressed in gray. He hadn't been able to see the man's face because his head was turned.

As Harry watched the cloud tower, it decreased in intensity and rolled off across the horizon like a summer thunder shower concealing the presence of the time travelers with a mask of rain and isolated stalks of branched lightning. As he watched, there was a second flash of lightning and as his eyes traced its path to the earth, he saw illuminated beneath it, a large old wooden house high on a hill. As Harry approached, he smelled salt in the air and he quickened his pace because he knew that the sea could not be far away. He could smell it and see the fog rising in the distance beyond the old house. In between the intermittent bursts of light, it was very dark and he could see nothing, but then another blast of explosive light would illuminate the horizon and the house would stand like an adulterer suddenly exposed beneath the burst of a photographer's flash. It was a familiar old place and as he approached obliquely from the rear, Harry could see a glow from the front of the house illuminating the yard. As he came around the side of the house, he stopped short. There, spread out across the front of the house, in the yard, were five men. They had their backs to him and they appeared to be totally nude. He waited for one of them to turn, for surely they had heard him kicking across the grass approaching the house. None of them moved a muscle. They stood about waist high in the blowing grass, their naked bodies seemingly frozen in mid-stride. As he approached, Harry noted that they stood in positions of quiet reflection, pensively, as if struck dumb and frozen in time by the sudden realization of one thing or another.

The five appeared to be sculpted from some soft fine stone or molded from smooth river clay and baked brown in the light of the golden sun. But these were indeed living entities, as he was able to confirm by watching the slow but steady rise and fall of their chests. These must be questors like myself, Harry thought. At one time in the distant past, each and every one must have been clothed in the specific fashion of a particular age, denoting his place in time and point of origin. He walked around looking closely at the five men. Apparently they had been standing for such a long time at their lonely vigil, that they had become as statues. Perhaps, he thought, they have been standing so long that the very molecules, which constituted the fabric of their individual costumes, have ceased to spin out of boredom and finally sloughed off into some other probable reality where their efforts, might be, if not needed, at least better appreciated.

Although they were physically different in stature and age as well as skin hue and musculature, each had a similar facial expression. It was as if someone had just whispered the punch line to a grand and glorious joke into their ear. They looked as if they were captured in amber at the very edge of open laughter. It was evident in the slight puckering at the corners of their mouths and in the fine wrinkled lines that folded back and about the corners of their clear sparkling eyes. Their eyes were open, colorless and brilliant like faceted stones. Their eyes were fixed open without the slightest motion, seemingly focused on eternity but with a deep sparkle of inner realization that had somehow brought them to the very edge of open laughter and then left them suspended, mid-stride, to consider their last thought for a while, perhaps forever. But then again, maybe they would all waken momentarily and proceed on about their business. Like still photographs fixed in a dish of developer, they just seemed to float there and stare out but with an inner life and light, as well as a slight, but unmistakable smile that played around the edges and threatened to become contagious.

These must be the *Standing Dead* mentioned by the *Geni of Desire*, Harry reflected. These must be the ones who made it to the edge of the *Big Sea* and no further. The yellow, the brown, the black, the red and the white: the five races that were man. These were preserved along with the old house as a reminder that while some things work, others don't. This much he remembered, but as he turned toward the house, there seemed to be much that he was still forgetting.

There was light coming from the front of the house and through the windows Harry could see many candles burning in the chandelier. He approached the house and climbed the stairs. At the door, he turned, his senses captured momentarily by the strong salt smell of the sea. Beyond the *Standing Dead*, he could see nothing but the formless whitish mist that contained the ocean, the *Great Surround*. As he turned into the house, he felt no rush of excitement or great sense of expectation, only curiosity. Harry couldn't recall ever having been in the house before and yet everything it contained seemed supremely familiar. There was a chandelier full of candlelight and an ornately carved wooden table situated directly beneath it, and upon the table, a crystal punch bowl...

***

Down the hall, in a rather small cheerless, gray, sleeping room an old man stood leaning against a mantle-piece looking at his own reflection in a wide oval mirror.

"It's time to go, love," said the old female friendly. "We have many, many other places to be."

Harry raised his eyes. Reflected within the mirror's silvery surface were nineteen human faces, both male and female, young and old. They were nodding and smiling, ready to depart. Their two-hour tour of the last wooden house in *San Francisco* was over. Harry continued to stare into the shiny reflective surface of the *see--into the eyes of a dreamer*.

"Are we ready, Harry?" said their guide with the merest hint of a smile.

Harry turned from the mirror and looked at them all smiling. *"Oh, what flowers of delight!"* he said.

And then, they were gone, like hot grains of sand on a Fall wind looking for the Moon; zooming through the *Great Surround*, cutting through the liquid like a knife of *Light*. The whole group was moving through the water at great speed and the sea was playing the tiny ridges of nerve that lay just below the surface of his skin as if he were a record and the ocean one vast phonograph. As he felt his long smooth body break the surface and launch itself skyward in a high graceful arc, he observed the sea spread out before him in all directions. Ecstasy would hardly express the feeling that filled him and then, as the momentum which had carried him skyward ceased, and he began his descent, Harry turned his head ever so slightly, and there, directly below him was the white dolphin, a reflection, upon the smooth clear surface of the sea.

At that very instant Harry let out a great human gasp! And then the image of the white dolphin froze as if it were the last frame of a movie and the color slowly leached out of the picture until it was merely a sepia tone still photograph

As the *camera* pulls back we can see that the frame is the curtain in a movie theater. The camera pulls back even further as the lights come up and we see that the camera is in the audience. The couple in front of the camera stand and turn to leave and we see that it is Harry and Asher in modern dress.

As they progress up the aisle, through the crowd, we see that all of the characters from the story are now members of the movie audience. But they are unaware of the parts they have played, unaware of the lives they have lived, unaware of Harry and unaware of Asher, unaware of each other. Merely anonymous members of a crowd leaving a movie theater.

As the ending title credits roll over the sepia toned still image of a dolphin leaping high above the water, Harry and Asher move through the crowd across the lobby and finally out into the street. The movie theater is in an attractive small American town. It is a summer's evening. As we see them exit the theater they casually glance at one another. There is clarity in their eyes and a secret sharing in their half smiles. As they cross the deserted street they approach a white van. On top of the van are two clear ocean kayaks.

***

The Catcher of Words finished his story, looked at those of us gathered around the fire and smiled mysteriously. We smiled at one another and nodded. We had enjoyed his story of the white dolphin who dreamed itself a human being. The *Teller of Tales* moved his Eagle feather once more over the coals and then asked us to look away, as he was about to leave. We did as he suggested and when we looked up again he was nowhere to be seen, and there were no footprints in the sand, but the large fin of a full grown Orca was observed silently gliding away in the distance. Nothing further was said. This night would become a treasured memory. This had been the night that the *Catcher of Words*, the *Teller of Tales*, the *Shape Shifter* had come to our fire and spoke of things yet to come. Of probable realities; of things that never were but might have been, and yet still could be.

THE END

Made in the USA
San Bernardino, CA
15 April 2014